Effie and Her Friends
A Story of Friendship

ROBERT E. MONEY

© 2019

Published in the United States by Nurturing Faith Inc., Macon GA,
www.nurturingfaith.net.

Library of Congress Cataloging-in-Publication Data is available.

ISBN 978-1-63528-068-5

Cover photo: Diane079F

The time: the forties and fifties

The place: South Alabama

"Effie, my older brothers say that God made boy cardinals more special than girl cardinals. Is that true?"

Effie's reply: "God *did* make boy cardinals more colorful. Color does not make you better; it makes you different."

Dedicated to Coy J. Money, a brother whose heart, head, hands, and feet worked with such precision. To walk with Coy was to keep company with Jesus.

Contents

Preface

Some say you can't go home again. I believe not only that you *can* but that it is essential that you *do*. In *Effie and Her Friends* I journey home again and unpack some treasures that were stored away in the attic of my childhood memories.

Effie was a childhood friend who was poor, black, and crippled. Our emerging friendship, much like our faith, pushed against and crossed over barriers of race, sex, and social status. My journey home through the memories I share captures the gentle, growing friendship between a girl and a boy, a black and a white, a child of a tenant farmer and a child of an owner.

Each of the twenty episodes, like an open window, provides more and more light and allows a soft, steady breeze to blow in across our friendship. It is a friendship that quietly, yet openly, teaches personal Christian qualities such as respecting differences, sharing, empathizing, remembering, caring, fostering self-worth and self-confidence.

In *Effie and Her Friends* my childhood experiences are recounted and retold by my seeking, nurturing, thinking adult. The writings are childhood experiences viewed through an adult's perspective. Some parts of the story are told as they actually occurred. Other parts are told as a small boy wished them to be.

In remembering, I first found Effie hidden away in the distant memories of my past. As I began to write, she slowly walked out of the shadows of the woods into the open sunlight of the verdant, green meadow that lay beside her house and in front of mine. In sharing her with you, both she and I are alive in a new and different way.

It is a real joy for me to introduce you to my good friend, Effie. You will enjoy her as much as I.

Rainbows and Storms

Differences

With the loss of childhood innocence, adults take the differences from which children create rainbows and make them into storms.

[You] have put on the new self, which is being renewed in knowledge in the image of its Creator. Here there is no Greek or Jew, circumcised or uncircumcised, barbarian, Scythian, slave or free, but Christ is all and is in all. (Colossians 3:10–11)

There is neither Jew nor Greek, slave nor free, male nor female, for you are all one in Christ Jesus. (Galatians 3:28)

God has combined the members of the body so that there should be no division in the body, but that its parts should have equal concern for each other. If one part suffers, every part suffers with it; if one part is honored, every part rejoices with it. (1 Corinthians 12:24–26)

The open field in front of our house gave way to a dark green backdrop as the airy, grassy meadow ran flush up against the thick darkness of the undisturbed woods. It was a peaceful sight to sit on the porch and watch the cows graze off the plush, grassy table. The crows circled high above or waited anxiously in the nearby trees for some food of their own in the cow drops that we dodged but they found.

The forest that drew from the stream flowing through and beneath it also protected and shaded the stream. The forest and the stream were a happy pair because the strength of one was the joy of the other. The trees grew tall and wide, stretching out their arms so that their fingers met, forming a never-ending archway through which the stream flowed like a bride moving toward her groom, eager to join the river to become one.

The forest at the foot of the meadow served as assurance for me. Like the sameness of the morning, I always found the forest in place and waiting. It was a mixture of oaks and pines, sweetgums and poplars. In my imagination the pines were the tall, agile centers and the oaks were the strong, towering linemen who preferred football. Underneath were the scrubby oaks and the seedling pines that would make up the team of tomorrow if left alone to grow and mature to treehood.

Even though the forest was always there, it had an ever-changing personality. In the summer it was fully dressed in varying shades of green. Each branch was softly layered with full-grown leaves. Together the branches formed an unending umbrella that held back the heat of the noonday sun. A cool breeze softly blew through its shadows, and the waters of the creek cut through its shade. In the summer the forest was at its best. It had just finished giving birth. It had not yet begun to die. Summer was its moment to live!

Summer had its way of slowly blending into fall. The forest and our guest room bed usually changed colors about the same time. The light green blanket of summer that lay undisturbed til company came was removed and replaced by Mom's heavy quilt with hundreds of red, yellow, gold, and brown patches. The change of the forest from summer to fall came so slowly that I was always surprised by its appearance.

Then winter came, and the forest stood almost naked. The trees looked so bare and gray, depressed for losing all their investment of the past season, yet hopeful, knowing another season was on its way.

And sure enough it was! The nudeness of the winter dressed slowly with new growth. The forest, at first dressed in the light green of spring, slowly turned darker as the dress became a darker and richer green. Spring, much like fall, had its mixture too. Dogwoods sat like placemat doilies and the sweet honeysuckles like pink napkins on Mother's dressed-up table.

It was to this forest that Effie and I would go when the heat of summer reached its peak. Effie, the daughter of Ease and Panella, a black family who lived on our farm, was older than I. When I was younger, Effie sat and played with me while Mama did her chores, canned peas and corn, or made her eight-day cucumber pickles. As I grew older and had no need for a sitter, Effie and I became friends. As we played, fantasizing and exploring, we slowly grew up and grew together. We chased lightning bugs and dug doodlebugs. We picked plums and caught minnows. We made fantasies out of fluffy clouds and experimented with smoking rabbit tobacco. We often went to the forest to seek out treasures and to play with many toys.

It was a typically hot and humid South Alabama day—the kind that made one search for a shady place. Effie and I knew where to find just the place to rest and play. On the way into the forest, we picked flowers from the honeysuckle bush and treated ourselves to their sweet, syrupy juice. We were startled by the rustling of the branches caused by the cows seeking a cool retreat in its shades and shadows. The birds darted in and out, up and down, looking for insects that felt safer in the forest than in the open fields. After a full, delicious meal the birds would rest on the tender branches that swayed in the soft breeze, and they filled the woods with the sounds of music. Each time we came, there were the predictables that assured us and the new creations that surprised and entertained us. This day we would find an unexpected surprise!

Effie and I moved through the darkness of the shade, stepping in puddles of light from the sun that sneaked through the tiny openings in the ceiling above. We wove our way through the maze of underbrush that grew thicker by the branch, moving toward an opening that we knew was there long before we saw it. We stepped from the thick underbrush onto a sandbar that was fresh and clean. The sand molded to the shapes of our feet, leaving footprints that were unmistakably hers and mine. Standing there in the presence of a stream that was both going and coming, we cupped our hands and lifted the cool, clean water above our heads. We slowly opened our cupped hands, and the water bounded off our heads. Some fell quickly to the ground. Some ran down our necks and skipped across our shoulders, crawling slowly down our backs like a thin piece of ice slipped underneath one's shirt. Refreshed, we sat to rest, not knowing a surprise was on its way!

The main stream moved swiftly through the cut channel that had been formed over time. On either side were the sandy, shallow places. The stream, tired from its hasty journey, would cut out to take a break before rejoining the waters that were more intent on catching the river and finally reaching the ocean, the finish line. The calm waters that hovered over the sandbar formed a smooth surface, like an ice rink on which skaters weave and dance to their own music. Skating easily and with amazing speed at times, water bugs entertained. We sat silently, not wanting to disturb or distract the performers. Each skater danced and wove its own intricate pattern, using the full rink to twist and turn, to dance slowly, and to move with incredible speed.

Water bugs dance best when there is no audience. Some slight movement on our part caused them to move backstage. This special gift of the forest we packaged away in our memory, knowing we could return to it when we needed to be entertained.

The sand on which we sat was soft yet firm like one of Mom's old sofas that served as a place to nap or as an additional bed for one of us when cousins came for a visit. Effie and I leaned slowly back until our bodies lay firm against the warm, soft sand. Our feet and toes felt the tingling of the cool, steady current. We moved our toes back and forth as if to say hello or bid goodbye to the water that flowed but never stopped. Looking upward through the slightly parted ceiling of the forest, we could see blue sky and fluffy clouds. The leaves that formed a solid front were slightly and briefly separated by a steady but lazy breeze. The narrow openings allowed us to peep, not gaze, at the sky above. No forms appeared. We had no need for fantasy. We were too blessed by what was to have any need to create what could be. Lingering, not escaping, was our present intention.

As we lay silently, thinking, a question I had often thought but never asked returned to my head. Close as we were, best of friends, I always felt hesitant to ask Effie such a personal question. At this point I was not clear about my rights, she black and I white, even in the safety of our friendship. Each time the question came, I would be eager to ask it, then hesitant, and finally I would send it away, knowing it would return. Today when it came, I felt the same hesitancy but was too safe to let it slip away. "Effie," I asked, "Why does Panella never dress or leave the house? Why does she sit back in the shadows on the porch where I hear her voice but never see her face?"

Effie took the question in full stride, not flinching or moving any part of her body to another position. My fear calmed by her reception, she easily replied, "Ma likes to be home. She is afraid to get out. She likes to stay in bed or sit in the darkness of her room. We take life to her, what she wants, what she needs. She never was one to get out much. After me there was another, a little brother named Mo. Pa always wanted a boy. He had a hard time getting born. He lived a few days and died. He was buried in a shoebox underneath the great big oak with its outstretched arms. She always felt that he was safe there. Since Mo died, Ma feels more comfortable in the dark. She says a big, dark cloud lives inside her."

"I'm sorry," I said. "Hope it was all right for me to ask. My mom likes to dress, to go, and to visit. I didn't know why your mom was different from mine."

The silence returned. We lay more still than usual. Then, as if we were hinged at the waist, we sat up, looking outward instead of upward. Our surprise was about to turn the corner, but we didn't know it. We only saw what was, and that was enough. Yet the forest and the stream were always fetching some surprises for us.

Effie and I sat still, observing all that was available. Then a cardinal, dressed in his finest, flew down from a limb on which he had perched for a rest and stood suspiciously on the yellow sand, checking, observing, and watching. Deciding that he was safe, he moved closer to the puddle of water that was off to the side. There in open daylight, in front of us, with no modesty at all, he bathed, dried himself off, dipped his beak repeatedly in the water, and drank until he was sufficiently satisfied. He spread his wings and lifted himself up to a low-hanging limb above the water. He sat there until his feathers were completely dry and then flew away, aware of our presence but too proud to acknowledge it. We wondered where he went, but we did not dwell on his plans. Two things were evident—he was well-dressed and clean.

"My older brothers say that boy cardinals are more special than girl cardinals, Effie. Is that true?" I knew Effie would know and she would tell me the truth. Sometimes my brothers made things fit, like pants they had outgrown but would not give up to the next one in line. Since they were big boys and they said boy cardinals were more special, I wondered whether "truth" was from them or from God.

"God *did* make boy cardinals more colorful. They almost shine, they are so red. That doesn't make them more special, though, 'cause each one of them was born from an egg that the mother laid. Without us girls, there wouldn't be any boy cardinals. Boy and girl cardinals are different, not better. Color is not enough to make you better."

It was time to go. Effie and I had seen only part of what the forest had to offer, but it was enough for now. We came to rest, to cool our feet, to put away our imaginations, to sit and watch the players of the forest entertain us with their show. Without intending it, we came to let our friendship grow. As we got ready to go, we knew we would be back. There was no grief, just satisfaction that we had been in the forest, a favorite place to be with a friend to sit, to watch, to be.

As I quickly surveyed the scene before leaving, the surprise that had been on the way appeared. "Look Effie," I said, as it floated hurriedly around the curve in the midst of the stream. It was moving at a steady pace, carried by the strength of current. But as it reached the sandbar, it gracefully left the stream and moved over to the water that hovered above the sandbar, resting a moment before it joined the fast pace of the stream again. On an open stage, with only a prop or two, there appeared two dancers, moving to the same music, hand in hand, never breaking, just turning and twisting to the music of the stream. They made one full swing around the stage, came back to the center, and almost exited before deciding to make one last turn. A dark brown leaf from an overhanging oak and a white blossom from a dogwood tree had met in the stream somewhere up above. The stem of the thin oak leaf lay snugly in the palm of the dogwood blossom. As the current pulled the dancers to itself and carried them out of reach and sight, Effie and I walked away silently, her hand softly touching my shoulder.

Ease

Power

It is one thing to hurt when you want something for yourself and can't have it. It is a far greater hurt to want something for someone you dearly love and not be able to give it. That is real impotence.

But we have this treasure in jars of clay.... We are hard pressed on every side, but not crushed; perplexed, but not in despair; persecuted, but not abandoned; struck down, but not destroyed.... So then, death is at work in us, but life is at work in you. (2 Corinthians 4:7–9, 12)

The purposes of a man's heart are deep waters, but a man of understanding draws them out. (Proverbs 20:5)

The glory of young men is their strength, gray hair the splendor of the old. (Proverbs 20:29)

Effie was my childhood friend. Ease was my grownup friend. He was old all the time I knew him, but he never got older! He was like God—the same yesterday, today, and forever.

Ease was Effie's father and my dad's best helper. He was a generalist, not a specialist. He could do anything. He could make a mule walk straight and pull hard; he could lift a heavy load with such little effort; he could mend a fence aged by time or injured by a rowdy cow or a misdirected horse; he could pick cotton with both hands, stooping endlessly as he worked his way down long, thick rows; he could chew big and spit far; he could empty a big orange soda or a royal crown cola in one lift; he could hoe peanuts and cotton like a skilled surgeon, removing diseased tissues without injuring the healthy organs. He cut away the weeds and grass and left the new plants intact and free to grow; he could look rough and dirty, but on Sunday he would look clean and handsome. As a husband he was lacking, so my older brothers say, and as a father he was distant yet gentle.

My father treated Ease as a person in some ways but as less than a person in many other ways. He climbed the back steps and entered through the back door when he came to fix a faucet or deliver the peas and butter beans he had picked. Even though they were near the same age, Ease said "yes, sir" and "no, sir" to my father. There were two water jugs. He drank out of one and my dad the other. When he did eat with us, he sat under a shade tree or on the back porch. Even though he was older, when the cab of the truck was full of children, Ease climbed over the raised tailgate and sat in the bed of the truck. If he were unhappy with being second or last, he never showed it.

Ease wore long-sleeved shirts and overalls and was seldom caught without a red bandanna handkerchief either neatly tucked inside his right back pocket or tied firmly around his neck. It seldom stayed long in either place. It was used to wipe away the sweat that beaded on his forehead or streaked down his nose, over his cheek, and puddled in the deep indention at the base of his neck.

To my father, Ease was a hired helper; to my mother, he was the fixer my dad was not; to my brothers, Ease was their pal; to me, he was my adult companion. He was old enough to be respected and experienced enough to be helpful. Most of the time he was sociable and approachable. My older brothers teased Ease about his sexual prowess and taunted him with unexpected grabs or jabs beneath his arms and down his sides. To be tickled was what he hated most and what my brothers liked best. Ease worked hard to stay protected, and my brothers connived and looked for moments when he was most vulnerable. Each time they won and he lost, my brothers laughed and Ease let out his signature expression, a "god-durn-it" that rolled off his lips and sounded like loud thunder after a sharp bolt of lightning. Its slow, guttural sound created long, loud laughter, and it was a sure sign that my brothers had scored again!

There was a question about Ease's sexual activity that Ease always answered but that my brothers could neither fathom nor accept. He declared repeatedly to my persistent brothers that he was "finished." The past was no more. His sexual power was gone. He would frequently declare in a language they understood but refused to accept, "What can't get up, can't get out!" Sometimes his declaration was accompanied by a slight grin and at other times with a mumbling growl. "No way!" said my older brother Knocker, as if he were defending something of his own. For Ease no present power made the active past too distant and far less interesting. For him it was history made but not revisited. I was too young to understand either the question or the answer. I was aware that the subject, like work, was daily and, like work, was never finished. For Ease it was pain. For my brothers it was one way to satisfy their growing curiosity about sex.

On the farm, sex is more out in the open yet seldom discussed. It's one thing to observe the animals. It's another to talk about one's own emerging sexual needs and interest with an adult. For my brothers Ease was a sexual treasure house. They found a freedom with Ease that they dared not use with my father. He held all kinds of secrets that my brothers persisted in knowing; Ease held the key. He was as persistent in keeping the secrets as my brothers were in knowing them.

Like children at Christmas, whose impatience finally peaks, my brothers were too curious to wait for their own discoveries. Ease had a packaged gift that they wanted to open. They were eager to know what was inside and how it worked. Like a wrapped present, they slipped around to peep inside it. They shook it. They asked questions about it. The partial answers they got served to create even more questions. Like any approachable parent, questions are initially expected. Then those questions become annoying, and finally they are ignored or openly resisted. Ease at first was receptive, then interested, and finally irritated. He liked to be perceived by my brothers as virile and active, but his own pain drove him to be both honest with their questions and irritated by their persistence.

Ease, to me, was like a clock; he had an open face, but the parts were intricate and hidden. I liked Ease because his face was open and his parts mysterious. In some ways Ease was for me the part of my daddy that I wanted but could not have. My daddy was strong, capable, and demanding, but he was not approachable. I respected him, feared him, and in a distant, structured way I loved him. I knew he loved me. We were parent and child but not friends. Ease was my friend.

Knocker decided early in life that farming, not schooling, was a better choice for him. After repeated episodes of discipline at school, he walked home from school, and Dad removed him from the classroom. By fourth grade Knocker had had all the classroom instruction that he needed and certainly more than he wanted. For my dad, when you stopped or finished one thing, you automatically picked up another. Even though Knocker was only ten, he was skilled in driving and plowing, and the open fields became his new and better classroom. Farming was more pleasant, instructive, and productive for him.

Since Knocker was so young and small, Ease spent a great deal of his time being the adult that was not yet present in Knocker. Knocker was a skilled laborer at eleven, and Ease was the laborer hired to assist him. Knocker could plow a straight row or disc an open field, but he couldn't change the plows or lift the seeds and fertilizers. Ease did that.

It was to this dynamic duo that I was often assigned by my dad to work. He must have thought it was the best training school for a merging farmer. He just didn't know how my plans differed. Farming was the last call I could hear. Perhaps ministry was the choice that most fully protected me from my dad's expectations. Knocker taught me how to plow and plant. Ease taught me to distinguish between certain plows that were used for different crops. He taught me seeds and fertilizers. He taught me some of the fine arts of farming, like how to tilt the plows to plow deeper or even closer to the rows of corn or peanuts. He taught me that 666 on a bag of fertilizer was not the announcement of some biblical monster waiting to descend and destroy. Like a cereal box that has all the vitamins listed, those numbers showed the approximate mixtures of the chemicals in the fertilizer for enriching the soil for better crops.

Ease taught me the difference between Spanish peanuts and runners, between white silver queen corn for the table and the yellow corn for the cribs that Dad kept full for the hogs and the cattle. Ease was an expert on making sure the right seeds were chosen and planted for Dad's gardens that were carefully placed on Dad's selective spots scattered all over the farm. Early peas were planted first, and they were small and round. Crowder peas were dark and fat. Butter beans were both large and blue and small and green. Ease knew them all, and he seemed proud that he could teach me. Perhaps it was one of the few times in his life that he was the respected teacher.

In the garden spots my conversations with Ease were short and to the point. The rows were short, and the seeds in the planter needed to be changed in and out so that we followed Dad's strict planting rules. I learned mostly by watching. Planting the major crops—peanuts, corn, cotton, soybeans—offered a different setting where our conversations were longer and more detailed. The rows were longer, and the seeds were changed less often in the planter. I asked questions, and Ease gave me the answers. He was a confident teacher, and I was an attentive student.

After filling the deep, oversized planters with seeds and the fertilizer bins of several sacks of 6-6-6, we would sit in the shade of the old high-bodied truck or an oak or sweetgum tree and watch Knocker slowly fade into a smaller size as he drove the tractor away from us, planting the seeds in the freshly disked soil. He plowed rows that were arrow straight and endlessly long. I was amazed and impressed that one so young could plow so straight. He seemed satisfied with Dad's Farmall tractor and plant-ers filled with store-bought seeds and bins with strong, smelly fertilizer. There was no doubt. It was his classroom. He was both its teacher and the student.

My older brothers had less need to talk with Ease and draw on his years of experiences, especially his tour of duty in the army when he was stationed in France near my dad. They were more interested in his sexual history than his military history. They had learned from him that in his younger days he had enjoyed his travels, and they were interested in getting back into that more tightly closed treasure chest. They were not convinced that there were no more treasures to add to his full chest. Their persistence was fed by their own emerging manhood and by their uninformed bias that black men are wanderers much like horses looking for mares. Ease, more by insinuation than by direct admittance, indicated that his "wandering days were over" and that part of his life was a fading memory. To young men who were emerging, "days over" was unthinkable. Their curiosity kept the subject open.

For me, because of my own age and my friendship with Effie, there was a treasure, a mystery buried deep down inside of Ease in which I was more interested. I wanted to know more about Effie. My interest had increased after one short visit down under the hill.

It was a dark, rainy, cold day in early March. It was Saturday afternoon, and at our place Saturday afternoon was the only time, other than Sunday, when there was an acceptable lull in the demands of the farm and its master. On this brisk day I had time but no plans. Effie and I had an easy, natural way of filling time with something both interesting and mutually enjoyed. I put on my heavy jacket, for it was windy and cold. It was most likely that we would choose something outside. We seldom stayed inside her house. Panella liked it dark and closed off; she had no open windows in the wintertime. It was dark outside, but not nearly as dark as inside.

The cold weather and the anticipation of doing something fun with Effie made the short walk even shorter. It was a silent, hushed afternoon. The farm equipment was silent. The animals were stored away in the barn. There were no birds in the sky. Only the big water oaks were dressed. All the other trees were stark naked.

As I approached Effie's house, the same silence that filled my walk was there. No one was outside. The doors and windows were closed. The silence made me more cautious. I walked around the house to the front steps that led onto the porch where in the summer Panella sat frequently but silently. As I approached the steps, I saw that the door was slightly open. I climbed the steps and stood quietly on the porch. I saw Effie lying on her parents' bed. Ease was at her head, and her two older sisters, Queen and Kate, were at her side. My curiosity carried me nearer the door before I suddenly stopped. I froze in my shoes as if I had stepped into freshly laid concrete. I was too bound by the unexpected to go forward or back. I just stood there planted in my silent tracks.

Kate, who stood nearest the door, sensed my presence on the porch and put her finger to her lips, not to hush me but to confirm my presence. I felt a rush of relief, somewhat relaxed, and waited for Kate. It was only a few moments. Kate walked to the door, slid through its narrow opening, and walked out onto the porch. She reached out and gently but tightly took my arm and led me away from the door. It was obvious Kate did not want me to see Effie or Effie to see me.

Quietly, she said to me, "It's okay. Effie is all right. She just had one of her fits. She won't be able to play today. Come back tomorrow."

"Okay," I said softly, and I turned and walked away. The short trip up the hill was longer. Effie was going to be okay—Kate assured me of that—but what in the world is a fit?

Ease's library of life experiences was filled with many different types of books. My brothers seemed more interested in his autobiography on sex. I wanted to read his book on fits. My brothers checked out his sex book, read quickly, and moved on. A page at a time seemed sufficient. I had never checked out his book on fits. I didn't even know. I had known it was there for a long time. I didn't know the title. Now I did. Ease had never talked about it. Did that mean that he wouldn't? Or that he couldn't?

One of the things I had learned about Ease was that when he could not find an answer about something, he reached up and got God. It seemed that for him God could always tie up all sorts of boxes and packages with neat, strong, colorful ribbons. God was absent until needed. Sort of like my daddy. He had an answer but no explanation.

It was a hot, early summer day. The peanuts were breaking through the loose, airy soil in which they were planted. Fresh new sprouts were reaching up and out. Growth was their intent. Knocker was plowing and fertilizing at the same time. To grow, my mom believed that you had to be clean and fed—and in that order! Peanuts were the same. Plowing cleaned them, and fertilizing fed them.

Ease and I loaded Knocker up with some fresh water that we had fetched from the ever-running spring that fed our fish pond and filled our jugs for drink. The fertilizer bins were filled, and Knocker was off plowing rows that seemed to stretch for miles. Ease and I settled back in the shade of a large sweetgum tree. Immediately I thought about the book I wanted to check out. The permission to check out the book I wanted badly to read or hear Ease read to me was buried beneath thick layers of my own anxiety. Would he or could he? So I chose another.

"Why are those large, ugly-looking birds circling in the sky?" I asked. It was the time and the place for this question.

"Oh, those are buzzards," he answered, pointing to the sky. "Buzzards are a strange breed. They are one of the few of God's creatures that prefer the dead over the living. They circle in the sky with their piercing eyes searching on the ground, looking for something dead. Buzzards do not kill for their meals. They find things already dead. If they circle for a while and move on, they are looking, waiting! If they circle in place, they have found a table waiting their descent. They have found a meal, and they are ready to feast.

Buzzards have voracious appetites. I have known them to eat an entire cow in one setting. The only things left were the bones, and they were picked clean!

"Why do they eat dead things that stink?" I asked.

"God made 'em that way. It sure makes things nicer. It keeps the world from stinking up, and it helps find cows that don't come home at night. God likes differences 'cause God sho' made a lot of them! Some folks are tall, and some are short. Some are fat, and others are skinny. God made you white and me black. You live on top of the hill. I live under it. Cows don't take up with horses, and goats don't take up with sheep. Some of us have two good legs, and some just have one. Like Effie. God just likes things being different, and we have to accept that as good."

"Well, I don't like big, black buzzards. But I guess God does 'cause he made them, and they eat dead things. I wonder if they like being buzzards!"

The tractor and the driver that had looked so far away now were coming closer and getting bigger. It was like looking at things through my daddy's field glasses. Through one end things looked small and far away. Through the other end things looked bigger and closer. Knocker's arrival meant more work for Ease and me and the closure of the library.

The next day, things were different. It was a hot summer, and Dad had sent us to another field on the farm that had been tilled and was waiting to be planted. The field sat like one of Dad's heifers, ready to be seeded so there would be another crop to sell. Dad always liked to plant corn that would be used both for eating and for feeding. Knocker drove the tractor. Ease and I drove the truck. Knocker was always real careful with the first row because if it were straight, all the other rows would be also. We filled the planters with seeds, the bins with fertilizer, and off Knocker went, driving more slowly and carefully because of that first row.

It was mid-morning, and a big part of the field had been lined with slightly curved rows of corn, much like Effie's head when one of her sisters plaited her hair and covered it with hair corn rows. Fresh water from the spring never tasted so good, and the dark shade made the gentle breeze feel even cooler. The peanuts in the adjoining field were growing slowly, closing the white-sand distance between the rows. They formed a carpet of green with specks of yellow blossoms, making the entire field look like a blanket of flowers that I had seen on my Uncle Bill's casket. Since the ground was almost covered with the thick, green peanut vines, I walked more carefully, thinking of Mom's words: "Be careful where you walk, for this is the time of year for rattlesnakes."

Knocker was on his way back with empty bins and planters, ready for a refill of both. Thinking about snakes stirs up what's inside a little boy. There were lots of questions. There was not enough time to ask them. I sure thought them! If God is so great and so good, why did he make rattlesnakes? Or if they needed making, why did they bite with poison? How did Ease stay so calm when he was bit by one? I would have been so scared I would have died! Are little children the only ones afraid to die? And if God is so good, why does Effie have fits? It was this last question I most wanted to ask. This question was much like Sammy, our coon dog. He would leave and stay gone for a while but always come back.

It was near lunchtime. Ease had taught me to stand out in the open field and use my shadow to tell time. I looked down, and my body and my shadow were one, so I knew it was twelve o'clock. Knocker knew it was lunchtime too. He didn't have to check his shadow, though; he simply listened to the growls and roars of his stomach. He raised the plows on the tractor, drove it under a shady sweetgum tree, and switched off its loud, roaring motor. We all three sat in the cab of Daddy's flatbed truck, driving home for lunch, leaving a cloud of dust behind.

Boys are like cows when they are hungry; they come straight home. We dropped Ease off at his house under the hill. He seemed less hurried than we. Part of that was his place. The other was no hot, home-cooked meal waited for him. Maybe some leftover cold biscuits, some soda crackers, and some slices of hoop cheese. Ease seemed more interested in the rest than he did the meal. I knew what waited for my brother and me. Mom and Queen, our cooks, were the best. There would be field peas highly seasoned with some fat back; blue butterbeans; hot, crunchy, crusty cornbread; mashed potatoes; fried chicken; and one of Mom's famous cobblers made in her white enamel dish pan. The tea was cold and icy. It was made early and left in the freezer in Mom's milk bucket that was for tea at noon and milk for supper. She let it get just so cold that slivers of frozen tea would hold on to the sides of the bucket. You could have your tea with ice cubes or without.

I knew there would be plenty to eat. I wanted to ask Ease to eat at our house, but I didn't. I knew I couldn't. Ease was my friend, but he was black. And black at lunchtime was more important than friend.

When the fields were waiting to be planted, lunchtime was just for eating. We ate, refilled our water jug, and quickly pulled up in front of Ease's house. It didn't matter how much we rushed; we always waited for Ease. One thing about Ease was the same: he never got in a hurry. In regard to movement he marched to his own drum. I think he needed to be in charge of something. His time and his place were noticeably his. We didn't talk about lunches, and I was relieved. We drove most of the way back in silence. Knocker had to get in one question: "How was last night?"

"Shucks, man, what are you talking about? I done told you that horse is dead."

It was strange to me. What horse died? What can't get up? Knocker had his question and asked it. I had mine. What happens when Effie has one of her fits? But I kept it.

Knocker parked the truck at a different place. He needed the seeds and the fertilizer to be nearer the remaining area of the field left for planting. By parking the truck nearer to the last row planted, refills were faster and our work easier. The planted rows covered over half of the field. The rows were neat and straight, like the chenille spread on Mom's bed.

The only thing we lost was the shade tree. Now we had to sit in the shade of the truck.

Knocker was full and satisfied. Calm had returned to his stomach. The planters needed to be refilled with yellow corn seeds and the bins filled with fertilizer marked 6-12-6. "Come on, Ease. Don't move so slowly. If you had slept last night, you wouldn't be so slow today." Ease moved on as if he had not heard a word. Neither Knocker's curiosity nor the empty planters caused Ease to answer or to hurry. Ease was Ease. I, too, was stuffed with Mom's good meal, but my question left unasked was staying more and going less. It was like a gnawing hunger that grew and remained until satisfied. I wanted to ask, but I couldn't. I don't know if I were protecting Ease, myself, or my friendship with Effie. Adults may do better with what they know than with what they don't know, but I just wasn't sure about me.

Out of the corner of my eye, I saw something move. I turned and saw a beautiful red cardinal perched on one of the bigger limbs of a new pine sapling. Saplings grew profusely on every uncultivated parcel of land on our farm. The male cardinal, so brilliantly red, and the green needles of the pines quickly moved Christmas out of December into July. Not only was I struck by the cardinal's beauty, so red against the dark green, but I had developed a divine connection with God through the presence of the cardinal. For a small boy God's distance and power needed to be more present and visible. The cardinal was my favorite bird. When I needed a word or a sign from God; when I needed the presence of God to reassure or encourage me; when I needed to make a bold or daring move; I looked for God in the form of a cardinal. Honesty causes me to admit that one was not always present. I quickly forgot when it was absent but always remembered when I looked and found it there. It only takes a few cardinals to keep a deal with God!

One of the cardinals I do remember appeared the day Effie had her fit. It was the presence of the cardinal sitting and chirping in the chinaberry tree by her house as I walked away that was for me the rainbow I needed, assuring me that Effie and our friendship were protected by God's care. It was as if the cardinal were chirping, "It's okay. It's okay. It's okay."

Divine inspiration and human rationale are often sparring partners. They are not opponents — just friends who give balance and share responsibility in doing right and doing good. It might have been better, and it would have been easier for me to go with divine inspiration with the cardinal. My human fear of meddling in Ease's personal affairs, disturbing his ease, or knowing the truth hooked my anxiety and froze my voice. Lingering with my need to know, my first task was to check out the setting. I quickly noticed that the field was halfway planted. One side was neatly lined with long, straight rows. The other side was soft and flat. It was just a matter of hours before the entire field would be planted and my time with Ease would be disturbed by some other farm duty or task.

The center of the field was its longest part. The rows Knocker was planting looked to be forever. He would be gone for longer periods of time, giving me more access to Ease and my question. Time was my friend. Like the field waiting to be planted, my unanswered questions about Effie's fits needed only to be asked.

My first intention was to just blurt it out, but it wouldn't come. The setting was right. My confidence was up. Divine inspiration and human rationale had met to declare "time for birth." My question to my mom regarding the birth of my younger brothers was always met by the same answer: "When it's time. When it's time! When it's time!" It was time, and I knew it.

I leaned back against one of the sacks of fertilizer, dug my bare feet into the soft, cool sand, and looked straight at Ease. In a firm, inquiring voice I said, "Ease, can I ask you something?" Looking back at me as if I had learned from Knocker and was asking Knocker's question about his night life, Ease hesitantly nodded his head yes. "You have told me about the seeds and the fertilizer, the buzzards and the rattlesnakes. Is it true that Effie has fits? What is a fit?"

Ease did not react as if he had been startled. He did not turn away as if he were angry or embarrassed. He just looked at me and remained silent. The silence was not distracting, like silence can be. It was inviting and accepting. For Ease silence was the friend he needed to collect his words and tell me what he wanted me to know or what I could understand. Just as I was ready for the answer, he was ready for the question.

"Effie has been having fits—the doctor calls them 'seizures'—since she was about seven years old. The first one she had seemed to last for hours. It was in the middle of the night. There were lots of stars but no moon.

I remember how dark it was when Belle [Effie's sister] came and shook me in bed, crying, 'Pa. Pa, come quick. Something is bad wrong with Effie.' I lit the kerosene lamp as quickly as I could, for it was too dark to walk. I lifted the lantern so I could see and hurried from our room to hers to find Belle, Kate, and Pearl holding Effie down. Her body was jerking, her eyes were rolled back in her head, and blood was on her tightly closed lips. I remember feeling so scared and thinking that something had to be done, but what? I did what I had to do.

"I climbed up on the bed, straddled her legs with my body to keep her from kicking and twisting, and grabbed her shoulders with my hands to stop her jerking. I was afraid that she might drown in her own blood, so I knew I had to open her mouth. I asked Kate to hand me her hairbrush, and I forced the handle of the brush in her mouth. The handle of the brush kept her mouth open and kept her from biting her tongue. Just as quickly as it had begun, it ended. Effie was lost for a moment, as if she were in some deep, faraway trance. She finally looked at me but did not see me. Then her eyes focused, she looked straight at me and saw me, smiled, squeezed my hand as if to say, 'I'm back! It's all right now!'

"It's bad enough to have the questions," Ease continued. "It's even worse to have no answer. The next morning I told Kate to stay home from the field and to keep a close eye on Effie. I told Kate that if she has another one of her fits, do what I did and send Belle over to the peanut field next to Cliff's house to get me. Walking away that morning was a hard thing to do, but I had to work. After struggling inside all day, I said to Kate that night, 'I can't live without knowing. In the morning walk over to Cliff's and ask him if one of them can take us to see Dr. Shell in the morning.'

"It was Saturday morning, and I knew Dr. Shell saw patients for half a day. I dressed myself in my church clothes, woke Effie up, and Pearl helped her dress. We sat on the front porch for just a few minutes, and we heard the sound of Cliff's old truck as it climbed the clay hill below our house. We were standing by the edge of the field road when the truck appeared in sight with one of Cliff's older boys driving. We rode to town in silence. Effie and I didn't know what to say, and Billy didn't know what to ask.

"After a slow, steady drive to the clinic, Billy parked the truck. Effie and I got out. Billy stayed in the truck. In Dr. Creel's office there was a waiting room for the whites and one for the colored. We were the first ones there. I didn't see many cars, so there must not have been many whites. We waited and waited. About lunch time, after all the whites had been seen, a nurse in a white starched dress with an oddly shaped cap pinned to her head, opened the door, smiled, and said, 'Dr. Shell can see you now. Follow me.'

"The nurse took us to a small, tight room where we sat and waited. Waiting to face the truth is both comforting and frightening. Effie managed her fear because I was there. I managed mine 'cause the doctor was there. Finally, the door slowly opened, and Dr. Shell—a tall, thin man dressed in Sunday pants; a stiff, starched white shirt; a brightly colored bowtie; and a long white jacket—stepped in. 'Mr. Sampson,' he said, 'what can I do for you?'

"'It's Effie, my daughter,' I said. 'Something happened three nights ago I don't understand.' I told him what had happened to Effie. I could tell he was a good doctor. As I told him all the happenings, he looked at Effie with a warm face and tender eyes. Looking back at me he asked, 'Is this the first time?'

"'Yes,' I said.

"'Effie had a fit. We call them seizures. She has a disease called epilepsy. It's a bad thing to have. There is no cure for it. There are some medications to help. When she has a seizure, there are certain things to do. Hold her so that her flailing around keeps her from hurting herself. Get the wooden end of the brush in her mouth quickly to keep her from biting or, even worse, swallowing her tongue. It would stop the airflow and cause her to suffocate. Take this prescription, and get it filled at the drugstore up on the town square. Do what I have told you to do if and when she has another one, and bring her back to see me in three months.' I stopped by the window and paid my ten dollars. I left the office knowing what she had. I did not know if she would have another fit or if they would get worse. Effie already had a bad foot. Now she has fits."

At that moment I looked up from gazing at the small canyon I had dug with the tips of my toes and saw one big tear form in Ease's eye. When it was ready, it slowly left the pocket of his eye, trickled down his dark, ruddy cheek, and fell gently onto the bib of his worn, soiled overalls. At first the tear scared me. I thought there might be many others. I wanted to run down one of those long, straight rows into the safety of the distant woods. Another part of me wanted to rise, go over to Ease, and wrap my arms around his big, broad shoulders. But that was closer than I ought, so I just sat silently still and let the fear dissolve into nothingness. The tractor that had been for a long time so distant was now reappearing in its normal size. Knocker would soon be back, and everything would be as usual.

There was something that stayed with me long after the day was over. It is still with me today. Ease had taught me. It is one thing to hurt when you want something for yourself and can't have it. It is a far greater hurt to want something for someone you dearly love and not be able to give it. That is real impotence.

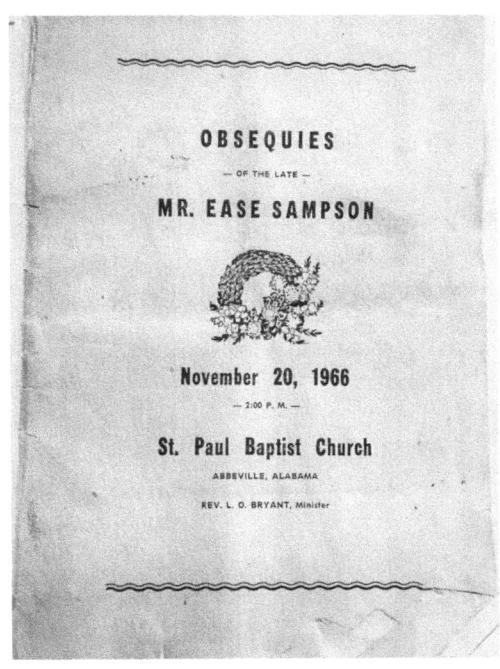

Little Bugs with Taillights

Security

In the presence of darkness, one tends to create what is not. In the presence of light, one tends to see what is.

A city on a hill cannot be hidden. Neither do people light a lamp and put it under a bowl. Instead they put it on its stand and it gives light to everyone in the house. (Matthew 5:14–15)

Light is sweet, and it pleases the eyes to see the sun. (Ecclesiastes 11:7)

For children, living in the country is a mixture of experiences and events that are predictable and yet unexpected. Some things are predictable, like spring, birthdays, and Christmas. Yet since they come and go, their return is kind of a surprise. That is the way it is with little bugs that fly around and burn their taillights.

In the early days of summer, these bugs always return, but for children who are gifted with the ability to wonder anew, the first flashing of a lightning bug is like something that has never happened before.

Effie and I liked to catch lightning bugs. Effie caught them with finesse; I caught them with speed. There is an art to catching lightning bugs, and Effie was my teacher. Effie treated each pursued and caught bug as if it were her child. She was as careful in the way she caught it as she was in her determined chase to catch. She had learned to be both good and careful at the same time. At first I was only good, not very careful.

One particular bug grabbed my attention, and I made it mine. There were plenty of others to choose from, but I wanted this one. Determined to catch my one, I did not run off in every direction, changing my choice based on the one closest. This particular one had darted out of the shadow of the trees and into the diminishing light of early evening. I could follow not only its occasional blinking light but also its moving form against the open sky. It flew above my head, out of reach, seeming to tease me with its wings. I zigzagged across the open field, pursuing with undistracted intention. Each time I closed the distance between us, waiting for its next move, the lightning bug would lift above my reach, and the chase would continue. I had more speed; it had more options.

The lightning bug moved along a steady line until, for some good reason (perhaps fatigue), it dipped and moved within my reach. I used my speed to get beneath it and quickly closed my palms together to form a cup. Trapped between my palms was my first captured lightning bug. Like a tiny flea trapped between Mama's thumb and finger, I took my captured prey to Effie. She had to patiently encourage me to open my cupped hands enough to reveal the catch. No way was one so evasive going to be set free. Effie had remembered her first catch, so she understood my hesitancy to offer any open space for escape. She also knew that between my palms was a lightning bug that was a casualty of my inexperience and my need to possess. Under her patient care and expertise, I yielded to her directions, separated my tightly cupped hands to create a slight opening, and peeped in to find that I had been successful in my pursuit. It was my very first.

Assured that the lightning bug was there and that it was trapped safely inside, I waited. Effie stood silently by as if to let me learn the art of catching and releasing lightning bugs. No blinking light. Just darkness! The slight opening became a wider space until my palms lay flat. There it was. Caught and captured but still no light. Effie made her move. Like a teacher who does not scold when one does not understand but sees an opportunity to share more truth, Effie said, "A lightning bug will not glow if it is scared or hurt. Let's let it go and catch another one." She lifted my catch from off my hand and laid it gently on the leaf of a low-hanging maple tree, like my mom often lifted my sleeping brothers from her arms and laid them on the soft pallet on the bedroom floor.

"Let's go again," she said. "This time let me show you how."

Effie chose another bug hovering near the ground, flashing its light like a plane coming in for a landing. From one step behind I watched every move she made. She cupped her hands and moved in close, then closer. With catlike quickness she opened her cup, scooped in her catch, closed her hands, and sat down at the base of a large water oak, leaning back to brace herself. She held her catch close to my searching eyes, parting her fingers to let in a little light. And there it was, crawling around captured but not hurt. "Keep looking," she said. "When it feels safe, it will blink its light." In my excitement and impatience I exclaimed, "Make it light! Make it light!" Waiting for what seemed like minutes when it was only seconds, the darkness that filled Effie's hands turned to light. "It did! It did!" I screamed. Effie gently opened her hands. The lightning bug crawled over her palm, down her finger, around to the underside of her long finger. Like a long runway at the airport, the lightning bug crawled down her finger and then used its wings to lift off and disappear. It joined the other friends in flight and sprinkled the darkness with periodic blinks of light. The teacher and the student spent the rest of the early evening chasing and catching little bugs with flashing taillights.

Each evening when the chores were done, Effie and I would meet in the open field between our houses to continue our game of hide and seek. Effie had taught me to put the bugs in a fruit jar that Mom had given me from her pantry. Inside the top was a lid that fit snugly over the jar.

Effie showed me how to use the ice pick to punch holes large enough for air but small enough to keep the bugs inside. That way the bugs could crawl, breathe, and even hide underneath the clover leaves that I picked from the pasture where the cows grazed. Safe inside, they would blink their lights as often as they did when they were free and in flight. It's one thing to see a sparkle; it's another to see a spray of multicolored lights shot from a Roman candle shoot across the sky. One bug is a miracle; a jarful is an unforgettable experience.

One evening when our playful hunt was at a lull and we were sitting on our concrete doorsteps, I asked Effie, "When did you learn to catch them? You are so good!" It was a question whose answer sat on top of her tongue ready to be shared. I could easily tell that she had a story to tell, and I wanted to hear it. Effie had good stories! As usual, she was slow to start. I just waited.

"At night it gets so dark in my house that I can't see my hand waving in front of my eyes. The sun slowly sinks behind the trees, leaving no lingering light; the moon is out so thin it looks like Pa has whittled it down with his sharp pocketknife; the darkness down under the hill sits so thick that little lightning bugs look like bright lanterns in the night.

"At your house you have electric lights, one hanging in each room. We have two kerosene lanterns. One stays in Ma and Pa's room. The other one moves from room to room, giving off enough light for each of us to wash off, undress, and put on our sleeping gowns. Pa tells us to save the kerosene, so there is little time between darkness and sleep.

"Kate and I sleep in the little bedroom off the front porch. Pa built it on to our house when Grandma came to live with us. It's not so dark when Kate is in my bed. I don't have to touch her to know she is there. I can hear her breathe or feel the warmth of her body next to mine. Knowing she is there is as good as having a light.

"One time, Kate left for a couple weeks. She went to stay with a white family over in Fort Gaines. The woman had a new baby and needed some paid help. Kate put all her dresses in one of the cardboard boxes Pa had saved. He likes to use boxes, not brown bags, to bring groceries home from the store. He keeps everything. 'You never know when it will come in handy,' he would say as the stack got higher and higher in the corner of the kitchen.

"While Kate was putting her stuff in the box, she talked about where she was going and what she would be doing. As she talked, I was thinking, 'It sure is dark at night! If she's gone, who will sleep with me?'

"Kate left early the next morning. The white man was waiting for her in his car. Kate picked up her box of clothes from off the bed, reached over and touched me on the arm, and told me to be a big girl. Thinking about the darkness, that was not what I wanted to hear. She walked down the front plank steps, opened the back door of the car, pushed her box across the seat, climbed in, and closed the door. As the car turned around in the yard, Kate's face looked only forward. She never turned and looked back. I watched as the car pulled away, staring at the back of her head as long as I could see. She was gone. Night was on the way.

"Pa and Ma thought I was old enough to sleep by myself. I was old enough to want them to believe that I could. I wanted to be a big girl more than they wanted me to be.

"There seemed to be more lightning bugs than usual. Maybe it was because I wanted them to be there! I sat on the porch in the early evening and watched as their brake lights blinked on and off. They looked like twinkling stars if you had been looking up rather than out.

"'Better get ready for bed,' said Pa, 'while there is some light.'

"I washed my face, slipped out of my clothes, unfolded my flour sack nightgown, pulled it over my shoulders, and shook my body 'til it fell down over my hips, covered my legs, and hung slightly off the floor. I threw the covers back and climbed in bed. I pulled the sheet over my shoulders and head, somehow feeling more protected from what might lurk in the darkness. The darkness became even darker. The last rays of sunshine faded softly away. I heard some old noises, but Kate was there. I heard some new ones, and Kate was gone! The old ones and the new ones made me feel more scared and made the night seem endless. I reached over to find Kate and remembered all those lightning bugs.

"The next day I couldn't help but think about the darkness. Since Kate was gone, I needed some other kind of light.

"Later in the day I looked for one of Ma's pint fruit jars, punched holes in the lid, screwed on the cap, and waited for the sun to set and the bugs to fly. My plan was to catch a few, place them in the jar, and set it by my bed on the turned-over nail keg that sat on Kate's side of the bed.

"In the late evening, knowing that darkness was on the way, I watched to see if and when the lightning bugs would fly. One by one they began to blink, piercing the darkening sky with light. Finally, one showed that had a bright blink. I followed its flight, never taking my eyes off of it. It darted up and down, within reach and then out of reach. It moved in and out of the plum bushes out by the barn. I waited until it was out in the open and within my reach and cupped it with my hands and carefully placed it in Ma's fruit jar. I had placed clover leaves from the field in the jar to settle its fears and satisfy its hunger. I continued my catch until I had filled the jar with eight or ten lightning bugs.

"I heard Pa cry out for all to hear, 'Bedtime!' I sat the jar on the nail keg, undressed, slipped on my gown, and pulled the sheet up around my shoulders 'til it was clean underneath my chin. I turned on my side, reached out for Kate, knowing she was not there, and kept my eyes on the jar, half-filled with clover leaves and my saving lights. Occasionally they would blink. For one split second the light would break the darkness, and all the things there during the day would appear, and all the things I thought might be there at night were gone. Greatly aided by my little friends, I went off to sleep, sleeping almost as good as when Kate was in my bed, by my side.

"Each night that Kate was gone, I let my old friends go and captured new ones. I slept by myself all the time Kate was gone, and Ma and Pa told me what a big girl I had become. I never told them about the light that dispels the darkness."

I told Effie I had to go. "Let's catch more lightning bugs tomorrow night." "Okay," she said. As I walked slowly up the hill, the covers of the darkness crept up over the head of the dropping sun. When I turned off the road and walked up the sandy driveway to my house, I saw the brightly burning lightbulb hanging down, dangling on the end of a yellow electric cord in the hall, and I thought of Effie and her lightning bugs.

Dreams or Fantasies

Imagination

The difference between a dream and a fantasy is the distance they sit from reality.

He wraps himself in light as with a garment. He stretches out in the heavens like a tent. He lays the beams of his upper chambers on their waters. He makes the clouds his chariot. He rides on the wings of the wind. (Psalm 104:2–3)

They will soar on wings like eagles; they will run and not grow weary; they will walk and not be faint. (Isaiah 40:31)

Fluffy clouds belong to each of us. They are ours to take and not to buy. They come and go. One has to play with them when they show. "A gift of grace, not of works, lest anyone should boast." The work comes in making them what you want them to be.

Effie and I had the perfect place to dream and to fantasize. The open field in front of my house and beside hers was bordered on all sides by massive hardwoods and tall, lanky pines. To the south were the woods that hovered above the quietly running creek. To the west was a line of massive, outstretched oaks with a sprinkling of tall, rangy pines. To the east was Effie's house, separated from the field by a thick collection of plum bushes and a line of pecan trees. To the north, up on the hill, was my house. Separating the field from our house was a row of Catawba trees and Dad's garden, which produced from early spring to late fall. My dad perfected the art of ongoing gardening!

Separating the garden from the clay dirt road that ran in front of our house was a line of Catawba trees Dad had planted to feed the Catawba worms we used for fishing. The Catawba trees stood in a line like soldiers dressed in army green. In the open field one lone tree was left growing where it had chosen to begin. It was a pecan tree, and it shared its special gifts in the late fall or early winter. It made a humongous shade for the cows to find rest after constantly grazing in the heat of the late morning sun. Some of the cows stood while others lay, chewing on their cuds. The shade of the tree was broad enough that often we and the cows stood, sat, or lay beneath its shade as common friends. Need has a way of equalizing God's creation. The cows knew us and we them. A few were too young and suspicious to stay. When we came close to the cows, they would walk or scurry away to find another shade tree just for cows.

The other gift of the shade tree was its fruits. The pecans were shared, and if one was too hard to crack, Effie would use her bigger, stronger hands to crush one pecan against the other. The cows were no threat to our treat, but their companions were. Dad wisely moved the hogs to another field in late fall so we could collect the pecans that fell to the ground either by natural process or hurried by the strong, gusty winds. We could eat 'til satisfied or gather them for selling to make some extra cash. Effie and I kept a little of the cash, but Dad kept most. The shade of the pecan tree was a place to rest and to dine. The open field was a place to lie on our backs to dream dreams and to create fantasies.

It was a cool autumn day. The need for sun was greater than the need for shade. On early days of fall or even in the midst of winter, when the temperature was low enough to make us shiver, Effie and I would seek the warmth of the sun. A pecan tree that had shed all its leaves offered a resting place to sit and lean and soak in the warming sun. The sun warmed us like mothers warm their babies while holding them close to nurse them at their breast. In the colder weather Effie and I got only the warmth. The babies got warmth and milk!

Sometimes we sat against the chimney of my house—protected from the cold, blowing breeze—and dozed or talked. Our houses were not made for warmth. They were a better fit for summer. The cracks around the windows and doors were wide enough for inside breezes. One of the foundational stones beneath Effie's house had shifted left, causing her house to sit more on its right. In my house the corner space in the room I shared with three older brothers, where the ceiling met the wall, offered us the opportunity from our bed to catch the moon on its climb or count as many stars as one could find from such a limited space. My brothers and I took great pride in claiming that we were the only ones who viewed the changing sky from underneath the covers of our beds.

For some on cool and breezy days, the house is where they go to get warm, to remove the goosebumps that show up on one's arms and legs. For us it was to the field—where breezes blow above your head, where the sun beams its rays to warm the earth and us, to chase away the chill. Our call was to the open field for dreaming dreams and framing fantasies.

It was to the woods Effie and I would go if we wanted to be entertained. We would sit by the creek and watch the water bugs skate with incredible speed and follow the dry leaf boats that floated on its surface, turning and twisting, moving downstream and out of sight unless delayed by a fallen branch or a snarly root; minnows played their game of hide and seek; birds fluttered in the water bathing and drinking; beavers worked endlessly to build their dam across the moving stream. The creek running through the woods with its off-course pools and yellowish sandbars offered a stage that changed its props but never drew its curtain.

The open field, another stage with front-row seats, gave us an unbroken view of the arching sky, dotted with pockets of scattered, fluffy clouds. There, we found a different kind of show. In this theater Effie and I were the actors. To be entertained is one kind of show. To entertain is another.

This particular play had several acts. It could not be rushed. The ground floor of the stage was grassy brown, firm and hard, with uncomfortable seats. Effie and I began to break the dog fennels, tall and baggy weeds, making two soft beds to lie on and look upward into the sky. Effie was an artist with so many skills, and she never used them all for herself. She broke more weeds than I and laid them at my spot 'til we both had beds the same. She knew that friends need space to honor differences and to give each the room to be.

It was a perfect day for framing fantasies. God, Effie, and I had worked to make it so. There were no clouds except the ones made especially for this show. White, fluffy clouds were scattered everywhere like someone had thrown handfuls of cotton against the distant, blue sky. They were there just waiting to be made into dreams and fantasies.

Lying there on our well-made beds of fennel, hands cupped like brown saucers to shield our eyes, gazing up into a bright blue sky, it was a day for dreaming dreams and sharing fantasies. The white cotton fluffs, pushed around by the soft, cool breeze, floated in and out of each other like a kaleidoscope, the shapes and forms ever changing. Some sat separately in the sky like the lone pecan tree. Others flocked together like families at reunions. Some appeared smooth as stones while others were jagged and broken like chunks of concrete.

Our friendship was so tight that Effie and I had established certain predictable patterns. Yet our friendship remained open, giving room for surprises. When we dreamed dreams and created fantasies, we were more predictable. I knew Effie's question would come first to seek my answer. In this game it wasn't so much her patient kindness that let me play first as it was her hesitancy to play. Her age had pushed her closer to the edge of adulthood, and her deprivation made dreaming more difficult. Fantasy was a favorite game of mine. I was a growing boy, no longer Mama's baby and not yet a little man. I was free to see things I wanted to see and to be whatever I wanted to be.

"What do you see?" Effie asked.

This question and Effie's asking it were as predictable as Mama's hand shaping biscuits for breakfast. I was so eager and ready to go that I wondered why she asked so slowly.

"A great big, flying horse with wings as wide as folding fans," I said. "Look, there it is!"

"Where?" she asked, searching the sky, looking to find what only I could see. That's the way it is with white, fluffy clouds and fantasy. What you see often has to be pointed out.

"See the great big fluffy cloud. It is the biggest one of all."

"I see that one," she said, pointing with her finger. "But it don't look like a horse!"

"Not that one," I quickly replied. "It's the other one. That's my horse with wings this wide," holding my arms as far apart as possible.

"I see! I see!" said Effie. "One wing is up, and the other one is down."

"Yeah! That's it!"

"Where will you fly?" she asked, knowing that fantasies tend to grow when shared.

"I don't want to go anywhere at first. I just want to fly." Effie was ready to listen, and I was primed to talk. My mind took off, and my fantasy kept up. I want to ride fast and long, up and down, to feel my stomach wheeze like it does when my older brothers drive real fast over thrill hill. I want to roll from side to side, tumbling through the clouds. I want to stand on my winged horse's back and dive into the deep blue water of the sky. Then up we go with unmeasured speed past clouds, through space, until we see the moon. Slow now, I whisper to my flying horse. Let's slow so I can see the man whose face is in the moon. He works for God, keeping watch over all of us at night, when day gives way to darkness. Shouting thanks for his watchful eye and good care, I leave him a basket of ripe, red apples to encourage his continued care.

Up and around the Little Dipper, through the Milky Way, on we ride. I see things up close that I'd only seen distantly so far when Dad and I would sit on the tailgate of his truck looking up into the starry night. Round and round we ride, like track stars racing around a track that never ends. Then we slow and float, marveling at God's beautiful creation that separates heaven from earth. Close, but no peek into heaven. God keeps that a secret so no one claims to know before they go.

Catch your breath! Rest a while. Get ready for a fast trip home. My horse can fly so fast I wanted to race a falling star to see which gets home first. "Home," I say to my winged horse. Faster than the speed of sound and skating water bugs, we ride past stars and the man in the moon. We hover over my house until my winged horse lays one of its wings against the ground to make a sliding board. I sit, then push, and slide right down, landing on my feet, standing on good earth. I wave goodbye as he lifts out of sight. I slip inside and jump in bed, staying awake so I can keep my fantasy in my head. The light begins to fade and slowly disappears like coals in a dying fire, going, going, gone.

Effie's dreams were like her doll. She had but one but dressed her in such different ways that only those who observed her carefully would know she was the same. It could be a big white house perched safely on a slopping hill; a field of flowers nodding to each other as if each one had been awarded first prize for its beauty and perfection; standing in the doorway of the rolling store with a handful of coins, asking the store man for crunchy chocolate candy bars, long-lasting Sugar Daddies, bubble-gum, moon pies, and R.C. Colas; standing tall and erect, looking dressed for church in a new white dress with bright blue borders.

Lying on her dog fennel bed, searching the sky, looking for the puffy clouds that held her dream, I knew she was searching hard to find just the right ones. Her delayed silence and scanning eyes told me that. "Look! There they are." Effie pointed to a group of clouds, not thick or cluttered, but closely scattered. Grouped in teams with equal sides, each cloud was free to run and shift, to dodge the ball and not get hit and have to leave the game. We had played this game too often for me not to see her dream. Effie with a crippled foot, not made but given, made her an easy target to be hit and have to leave the game. In choosing sides Effie was always last. In playing the game she was the first one out. In her dream she had good feet and was the last, not the first, to leave the game.

Fluffy clouds belong to all of us. People who have too little use clouds to dream dreams. Folks who have enough or too much use them to fanta-size. Dreams can be used for growth and change, fantasy for escape.

Baby Jesus and a Chocolate Cake

Empathy

It is not enough to describe a rose. Pick one! An ocean cannot be known by standing on its shore. Wade in! A tea cake is more than a smell. Eat one! How can God know man? Become one!

A gift well given is wrapped in eternity.

A gift opens the way for the giver and ushers him into the presence of the great. (Proverbs 18:16)

They opened their treasures and presented him with gifts of gold, and of incense, and of myrrh. (Matthew 2:11)

For us in the country, Christmas was more like a surprise visit from a distant cousin than an expected visit from the preacher during a protracted meeting. Much was said about the coming of the preacher. Little was said about the coming of Christmas.

Just like winter's appearance, there were some expected, predictable signs, but one had to be observant to notice and get prepared. The trees slowly disrobed, taking off layer by layer, until they stood nude, shivering in the cold. There were the burlap sacks hanging from the rafters in the hayloft of the barn, partially filled with tasty new potatoes that Dad had planted in spring and harvested in late summer or early fall, saved to give winter a taste of spring and summer. The clearest clue of winter's coming was the moving of Mama's flower shop from off the screened-in porch to the living room and all other places in the house that had room for her protected plants. In South Alabama snow was more of a miracle than Christmas!

We knew Christmas was on its way when the music coming from the radio by Daddy's bed began to mix in a few of the hymns of Jesus's birth and the songs about things we seldom or never saw like Frosty and sleigh rides. As the music mix became more and more seasonal songs, we knew the day was fast approaching. It was finally in sight when, on the day before Christmas, all the music was "happy holidays" or Jesus songs.

A few days before Christmas our house had a smell that lasted for a week, not just hours. My mom was better with cobblers than with cakes. Oftentimes the best part of lunch came after the pot of peas, the crusty cornbread, the fresh tomatoes and sweet nine-day cucumber pickles. The peach or apple cobbler, covered with light brown strips of rolled dough that let the juices bubble through, sat still cooling on Mama's oven door lid while we ate the wonderful preliminaries. When Mama brought it to the table, we had to clear a space for her large, white enamel pan that held her bubbling, brown-crusted cobbler.

Cobblers smell wonderful, but not even they smell like one of Mom's good layered cakes when lying on metal racks to cool before being stacked into one of her prized cakes. The good smell floated down the hall, out the windows, even to the porch. We could enjoy the smell but not touch or pinch and certainly not eat 'til Christmas Day. The yellow, thick cake dough made from scratch was poured into round pans, settling down before the dough began to rise. Like brothers eager to be tall, standing on their tiptoes, the dough began to climb 'til reaching full height. Under Mom's watchful eye, at just the right time, she would rescue the pans from the heated oven, let the pans sit to cool, and then carefully dump each cake on to the metal racks. Perfectly round and golden brown, they were stacked one on the other, each getting fully dressed with one of Mom's creative icings. One was pineapple, another lemon cheese, and always chocolate. The icing helped the layers to stack and stay and gave each cake an undeniable identity.

The icing was the source of the second good smell that floated up the hall and out the windows and was the mixture the artist used to paint each cake with color and taste. The cook-artist used a knife, a spoon, a spatula, or a folk to smooth and curl the icing on each layer and guide the icing down the sides until each cake was fully dressed in the color that perfectly matched its name: cherry, lemon, chocolate, and caramel. There were others known more by their taste than by their color. One cake, Mom's lane cake, was known to give a kick from some of Dad's whiskey, an ingredient in her handwritten recipe. To make sure the kick was strong enough, she drenched a cloth with whiskey before wrapping her lane cake to season and be just right for Christmas.

Each cake sat near the stove until it had cooled and the icing firmly crusted. One by one, each cake was carefully carried to the corner safe, where they were arranged according to size, shape, and color. The favorite ones were placed in the back to soften the temptation to touch or pinch. A thin mesh-screen backing on the two doors of her corner cabinet kept Mom's cakes in full view, allowed the cakes to breathe fresh air, and kept the kitchen mice from taking up residence at night when all was quiet and still. There was no sign, no lock and key, just an unspoken command— "no touch, no pinch, no cake 'til Christmas Day!"

As Christmas stepped slowly through the days of December, there was some talk, not much, about the two folks who show each Christmas morn. One was born in a barn. The other was never born; he just always existed! Jesus came from the East; Santa lived up North. Jesus was a special gift; Santa brought gifts to all good girls and boys. Jesus was one of us; Santa was all different from us. He had strange friends and helpers, like elves, and eight tiny reindeer and later one more with a bright red nose.

Jesus knew us well. He was born in a cow trough lined with clean, soft hay. He had friends more like us, people who tended sheep. He was born on a farm where there were sheep, cows, and mules. There must have been a dog and cat 'cause all farms have dogs and cats! When we heard the soft whispers of Santa and the tender words about baby Jesus, Christmas was just a day or two away.

It was a day inside the week of Christmas that Effie and I sat in the barn loft. December had some cold days, but this day was a mild one. We sat back from the opening of the loft to miss the stirring wind that made the temperature feel colder than the fifty degrees that registered on Dad's Pepsi thermometer nailed to the weathered wall where Dad hung all his farming tools. The loft was almost full of peanut hay. On rainy days the hayloft was a favorite place to play. We stacked the bales of hay in ways to make long, narrow tunnels through which we crawled and hid, playing the game of hide and seek.

Effie and I sat on two single bales of hay that had been left near the opening in the loft by my brothers when they got hay to feed the cows the day before. It was a good place to sit. Looking out the opening, you could see the house and watch Mom sweep the porch or pin wet clothes to the line that hung between two trees. The clothes would blow or flap in the breeze, dancing and drying at the same time. Dad would sometimes drive his pickup truck underneath us, pick up some tool he needed, and go on his way, never looking up to see if we were there. The cattle and the hogs went about their business, undisturbed by two folks who sat to talk about important things. It was like what God must do and feel, sitting and watching the world go on, undisturbed by his presence.

"Effie, does Christmas come to your house?" I curiously asked. It was a few days away, and I had seen no sign of Christmas at her house. There were no lights, no tree, and no smells of cakes cooking. I heard no music and saw no baby Jesus.

Effie answered my questions like she walked, slow and deliberate, never in a rush or a hurry: "Christmas comes, but we hardly know it's here. One Christmas I wanted a decorated tree. I went out by the plum bushes and found a little cedar tree, just a tiny fellow. I got Pa's long handled scoop and dug it up. I sat it firmly in a gallon green bean can that

I found out on the trash heap, packed it with fresh, moist dirt, and sat it on the front porch to decorate.

"I knew where there was a sweetgum tree, so I walked down the road toward the creek and gathered a small basket full of sweetgum balls that nestled underneath the tree. I had so many from which to choose that I had a hard time deciding. I filled my basket full so that when I got back to the porch, I could choose just the best ones to hang on my tiny cedar Christmas tree. I chose ten or twelve almost perfect ones with long stems still attached. I asked Ma for a few short pieces of her colored threads. I made a double knot, drew it tight around each stem, leaving enough thread to tie each ball to the branches of my little tree. Each tiny limb held a shoestring bow and a sweetgum ball. I kept it long after Christmas was gone, but not too long. I wanted my little tree, which for a while had been my Christmas tree, to be a growing cedar tree. I took it back where it had started, planted it in its own soil, watered it well, and checked weekly to make sure it had what it needed to grow. It's bigger than me now. Too big to be my Christmas tree!"

"Does your mom cook any cakes?" I asked.

Again hearing my question but in no hurry to answer, Effie finally broke the silence: "Ma don't cook at all anymore. Ever since she got that black cloud inside, about all she does is dress some days and sit on the couch, staring into space. Pa and I do the cooking mostly. Kate and Belle help out some. Ma never cooked special things like cakes at Christmas."

"My mom believes cakes are the most special thing. She, Aunt Mabel, and Aunt Donnie spend two or three days just cooking cakes. All kinds of cakes! She puts them in the corner safe. We have to look at them 'til Christmas Day. She believes that Christmas cakes can only be cut on Christmas Day. It doesn't make good sense to me to have more cake than you can eat on one day. Several slices are all I can eat. If we could eat cake before Christmas and after Christmas, we could eat slices of every cake. On Christmas Day cake is just one good thing we have.

"Mama has a great big, round, silver tray she made as a project in her home demonstration club. On Christmas Day when it's time for her cakes, she proudly brings that tray fully covered with slices of every cake. If there were a contest for kinds of cakes and quality of cakes, Mom would win a blue ribbon every year. When she brings in her tray, we give off oohs and aahs, and that seems to make her work seem worthwhile—a true gift of Christmas."

As Effie and I shared our stories about Christmas, something silently happened. Christmas seemed more present and the meaning of Christmas more real. The everyday-go-on-as-usual was softly penetrated by an air of expectancy. As we talked about the strange story about a birth of one so small and yet so great, the smell of hay and odor of the cow stalls rescued Christmas from the pages of a book and sat it down right in our midst. In the barn we could see it, touch it, feel it. Christmas does come in strange ways to strange places.

Effie broke our silence: "You know the little doll I own and care for and play with? My sister who lives away and hardly ever comes home brought it to me several years ago. It was a Christmas present. She brought all of us gifts. She brought Ma a white dress with blue flowers, hoping she would dress up and go to church. She brought Pa a brown suit that he wears every Sunday when we go to church at Saint Paul's Church. The doll she brought me has been like my child. I make her dresses from pieces of cloth from old shirts and dresses Ma stores away under her bed. I pretend to give her baths, and we talk. I teach her manners and sing her lullabies. She is the only baby I will ever have, so I take good care of her. She is my Christmas baby."

"Jesus was a Christmas baby too," I said. "I do not know why somebody so important had to be born in a barn. I was not born in a barn. You were not born in a barn. In Sunday school before big church, I see baby Jesus in those pictures lying in a trough of hay. Why was he born in a barn and not a house? Effie, do you know?"

"Yes, I do! Poor folks have to be born where they are. That's where Mary was, and that's where baby Jesus was born. If he had been born in a great big house or hospital bed, he might have been forgotten. Who he was made him special! Where he was born made him reachable! Poor shepherds ran far and fast to see him. Kings who lived far away sought him, found him, and brought him gifts. They brought baby Jesus soap to keep him clean, powder to make him smell good, and syrup to make him smile."

Effie and I finished our hayloft visit. We climbed down the sturdy ladder Dad had carefully nailed against the barn wall. I went off to my house to check out the cakes, and Effie walked down the hill to her house to check on Panella and her baby girl.

Thinking to myself as I walked toward the house, "We have all those cakes, and Effie has none," I turned to the left rather than the right to go behind the house, in the back door, past the kitchen to catch a glimpse of Mom's cabinet full of cakes. I walked back to the cabinet, opened the screen door, and counted. Twelve cakes! Not one was gone or pinched!

A light came on in my head. Talking to Effie about baby Jesus made what I was thinking and seeing so plain and real. Effie has no cake; we have twelve. It was Christmas Eve, and Mama was busy cleaning and cooking, getting ready for the day and for the big finale, the cutting of her cakes. Each cake would be carved perfectly and each slice arranged so that each cake stayed separate and not mixed in with the others.

Christmas Day was too late to execute my plan. Mom took up residence in the kitchen, and there was no way her presence and my plan could be in the kitchen at the same time. Christmas Eve was different. She mixed cleaning with cooking. It was her cleaning that took her out and brought me in to execute my plan that I knew was right when the light came on in my head.

The cakes were all in tip-top shape. No fingerprints or icing scraped away. No pinches. Each cake sat erect like Miss Tribby sat in church. Mama was more relaxed about the safety of her cakes and felt less need to keep a watchful eye. A quick passing glance assured my mom that all was well. She had no need at this time to take a head count.

In my boy-like thinking, I knew that if she missed just one of her many cakes, it was possible that the theft would be dealt with later. The spotlight could not shift to find a hiding thief at the very moment of her entrance from the wings, to stand stage center with her great big silver tray steadied on both her hands, weighted down by slices from all twelve of her cakes. She protected her special moment in time, the cutting and serving of her cakes.

I knew Mama would clean the front room, referred to as our guest room, for my older sister and her husband. The room was kept as a guest room by shifting out whichever child had moved in when an older one moved out. It was the front, best room, and each child progressed in that direction, gladly giving up a shared room for one of his own. When the older sibling came home for a visit, it was her room. Ownership had not changed just by being the next one to move in.

When the room was to have a guest, it was not just cleaned; it was perfected. Bed sheets changed, floors mopped, furniture dusted, windows cleaned, curtains washed and starched. I knew Mama was preoccupied for a time, gifting me with the time I needed to carefully execute my plot without leaving any noticeable evidence of disturbance.

I had found a white shoebox on a shelf in Mama's closet wide enough to hold a cake. I had seriously studied the cakes to see which one Effie would most like and Mama least miss. It was an easy decision. Effie liked chocolate, and Mom made several chocolate cakes, knowing it was our favorite too. Each was different but enough alike to keep Mom away from a count. The high-back chair mom used in the kitchen for resting gave me the height I wanted, and its back pressed against the safe gave me the safety I needed.

A thief had never been so prepared. I was more scared of being caught than I was feeling guilty about doing something wrong. Somehow, stealing to share eased the guilt but did little for my fear. To get caught messing with one of Mama's cakes carried automatic execution.

The cake fit perfectly in the box. It was a heavy, wide box that had housed Dad's new brogan shoes. I carried my stolen jewel carefully down the back porch steps, walked along the edge of the woods, and sat down on a bale of hay that lay close to the corn crib door, directly beneath the hayloft where Effie and I had sat talking about Christmas and baby Jesus. As I sat to rest, my fear still bubbling up and over, smelling the sweet peanut hay, with my gift close beside me, though my body was filled with fear, my heart was filled with love.

I was most assured that Mama was too busy to look outside. I grasped the box on either side, and with quickness in my steps, I walked down the hill to Effie's house. Her wooden windows were lifted and hooked in place. The door was slightly open, keeping out too much of the cool air but letting in some needed light. I knocked and loudly whispered, "Effie. Effie". As usual I waited for her slow, casual pace. The door finally opened, and Effie stood there, holding her baby in her arms. I sat the white box at her feet and said, "Baby Jesus and I thought everybody ought to have a cake for Christmas." As I turned and walked away and started my climb back up the hill, the glow of the candle in my heart was bright and warm enough to chase away the fear that Mama might discover that one of her cakes was missing.

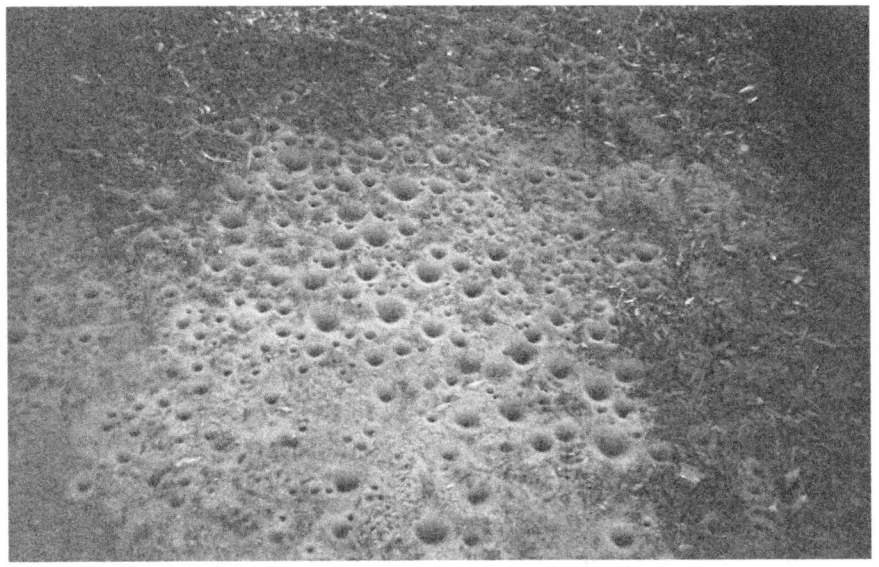

Doodlebugs

Kindness

When stirred gently and called kindly, one's fears, like doodlebugs, move upward and outward, leaving the darkness for the light.

An anxious heart weighs a man down, but a kind word cheers him up. (Proverbs 12:25)

Love is patient. Love is kind. (1 Corinthians 13:4)

There is no fear in love. But perfect love drives out fear. (1 John 4:18a)

One of the good things about having Effie as a friend was that she introduced me to her friends. She loved the world and all that was in it. She introduced me to her daffodil bulbs planted in their special place, waiting for the passing of winter and the presence of spring to rise up with their nodding heads, waiting to open with the first sign of spring; her growing cedar tree that had been her tiny Christmas tree was a favorite resting place for birds, and for a mockingbird a safe place to nest and lay her eggs; the long-stemmed purple violets that grew profusely in the damp soil beside the creek made bouquets for both our moms; her pet goat, Millie, gave her milk, and Effie returned the favor with affectionate hugs and rubs. Effie lived well in her world and made friends easily. I often wondered was it her heart, her crippled foot, her fits, her house under the hill? Or was it because she was poor and her world was the best gift she had? All I knew was that she didn't keep it to herself. She shared it with her friends.

Doodlebugs were one of her favorite friends, especially on rainy days. I had never searched for doodlebugs. Effie had! I had heard her hum and sing a song about doodlebugs but not when she was hunting for them.

One day, I sat in one of Mom's painted green rockers on the front porch, entertaining myself. The rain ran off the house, dredging out shallow trenches where it landed in the soft sand. The steady, misty-like rain of the day before had continued through the night and on into midmorning, cooling down the summer heat. A white fog rose out of the woods that bordered the cow pasture in front of the house. Each time I saw the fog climbing up through and over the thick trees, I remembered what my dad had often said as he sat with us on the front porch when rain gave us a respite from work. "Look," he would say, pointing his finger toward the fog. "The rabbits are cooking breakfast." This particular day, the rabbits were cooking a big breakfast! Fluffy, our dog, lay on the porch beside me. After a while I had had enough self- entertainment. Time to call on Effie!

I found Effie sitting on the floor in her bedroom. She sat in a pocket of light that had puddled on the floor. She was dressing her doll and combing her hair. Her mothering instincts were more active on rainy days. I sat in the open doorway watching Effie mother her child. She was a patient mother. Each stroke of the comb was firm but gentle. Dressed and groomed, Dolly stood leaning against the leg of a cane-bottomed chair. "Let's get some doodlebugs," Effie announced with haste and energy. She pulled herself up using the chair to support her climb and led us out of her room. I followed.

A doodlebug is a tiny, soft brown bug. It buries itself in the dry sand underneath the porch, deep enough to be protected yet shallow enough to quickly or slowly surface, based on how it is invited out. In your hands doodlebugs curl up into tiny balls, rolling around from side to side like shelled peas in a bucket.

Doodlebugs live in large families, but each one has its own private dwelling. All of their houses are built underneath the ground, yet it is easy to find where they live. The roofs on their houses are all the same. Each one has a perfectly formed circle that sits on top like a miniature volcano. Their houses sit side by side like one of the neighborhoods in town, close but enough space to be a single dwelling. They visit with one another underneath and with us when they come up and out.

Effie led the way. She bent down so as not to bump her head, crawled underneath the south side of her porch, near where Della and Belle slept. The north side of the house was blocked by large pieces of tin to keep the cold winter air from blowing underneath and rising up into the house from cracks in Effie's floor and chimney. The porch was tall enough so Effie and I could walk underneath by bending at the waist. Effie sat down where there were no circles in the sand and motioned for me to do the same. We sat quietly for a while, giving the doodlebugs time to get used to our presence or ready for a visit.

I liked for Effie to teach me something new. She was like Miss Tribby, my first-grade teacher. She never made me feel dumb because I didn't know how to do something or badly if I had added wrongly or misspelled a word. She showed me how to do something right or better. "Doodlebugs," said Effie, "are very watchful. They sense when something or someone is around. If they sense danger, they stay hidden or bury even deeper in the ground. If you call them calmly and softly and stir them gently, they come to the top. They are real cuddly and friendly."

"My sister, Belle, scares her doodlebugs. She cries out 'DOODLE-BUGS, DOODLEBUGS, YOUR HOUSE IS ON FIRE!' And she stirs like it is! Doodlebugs are smart, so instead of coming to Belle's call, they go deeper, not trusting the fire or Belle. I do it differently. I stir easily and call softly."

Effie searched until she found a long sage straw that had been part of her mother's broom. It had fallen through the crack in the floor. It laid there lifeless and helpless, ready to be used. Effie took it and began to stir. The straw was too brittle. She threw it aside. Looking further underneath the porch, she found a long, sturdy splinter that had broken off one of the planks in the porch. The splinter was both strong and sharp.

Finished with her talk, Effie was ready to demonstrate. My eyes were fixed on her every move. She was the teacher, and I was the student. I taught her how to shoot and play marbles. She was ready to teach me to call out doodlebugs. That was part of our good friendship. Both of us could teach, and both of us could learn.

Effie held the sharp splinter tightly between her right thumb and her pointin' finger. She turned her body slowly so that she sat directly in front of several doodlebug houses. She sat on her knees, balancing herself with her legs and feet behind her. She carefully stuck the sharp splinter in the center of the doodlebugs' roof.

Effie cleared her throat, and instead of crying, 'DOODLEBUG, DOODLEBUG, YOUR HOUSE IS ON FIRE!' she stirred and quietly whispered, "Doodlebug, doodlebug, your house is on fire." Then she created her own call: "Doodlebug, doodlebug, your friend is near. Doodlebug, doodlebug, no need to fear." Stirring and softly speaking, keeping her eyes fixed on the hole in the roof, she quickly broke into a successful smile. "There it is! There it is! See it!" Effie exclaimed. I moved closer and saw a tiny brown bug breaking through the soft sand. Effie picked it up, softly holding it between the thumb and finger used for stirring. She placed it in my open hand. It quickly rolled into a dusty, tight ball. Effie reached and rolled it back and forth in my hand as if she were rolling one of my prize marbles.

After letting me enjoy its presence for a little while, Effie took it from the palm of my hand and gently laid it back in its hole. It used its whole body to dig down through the loose, dry dirt and slowly disappeared. Knowing that I had held her bug, Effie wanted me to hold my own.

"Your time," Effie said as she turned and handed me the stirring stick. "Can I do it?" I asked with some fear and trepidation. Eager to try, I took the stick, held it tightly between my right thumb and pointin' finger, trying hard to do like Effie. In the excitement of my doodling and the fear of not finding one, my voice was loud and my stir strong. Without a scolding word but with her finger to her lips, Effie reached over and touched my hand. My voice and my stir both softened. Then, as if it could not wait, my very own doodlebug climbed to the top and pushed out of its roof. Both Effie and the doodlebug waited for me to pick it up. Reaching down, I carefully picked it up and placed it in my cupped hand and watched as it sat still and then began to roll as I moved my wrist from side to side.

"Can I keep it?" I asked Effie. "It's my first!" Effie was in a hard place, and I sensed it. She was trying to balance my excitement with the safety of her friend. She sat quietly for a moment, giving my excitement more time to be enjoyed. I wanted to keep my first ones, too. I put them in a jar with holes punched in the lid. I covered the bottom of the jar with dry, loose dirt. I turned the jar sideways to make their entry into the jar easy. I closed the jar tightly both for their safety and for my keep. I sat the jar on the nail keg beside our bed. I went to sleep, and so did they.

The next morning, I woke up and took the jar in my hand. Inside, I could see that they had crawled as deeply as they could. I thought they were resting on the bottom of the jar. I turned the jar and saw that they were not resting. All of them had died. The jar that I had made for their one-night home had become their grave. I took the jar and crawled back under the porch. I dug a hole for each of the bugs, laid each down, and covered each of them with dirt. On top I made a roof, like a volcano. Effie turned and said to me, "Doodlebugs are to be dug, not kept." Holding my first doodlebug, I studied it long and deep. I gently picked it up, sat it on the lip of its roof, and watched it dig down and disappear.

Doodlebugs were now not *her* friends but *our* friends. On rainy days Effie and I would sit underneath the porches of our houses. With rain falling steadily and softly, we would listen to the pitti-pat, pitti-pat of the rain falling on tin roofs. When listening needed to change to activity, we would find our sticks. Passing by our houses, you could hear a familiar duet: "Doodlebug, doodlebug, your friend is here. Doodlebug, doodlebug, you need not fear!" As we sang and dug and made new friends, Effie and I became even better friends.

Boat Races

Competition

In competitive games there is a winner and a loser. In friendship if there is a winner and a loser, the friendship always loses.

The race is not to the swift or the battle to the strong, nor does food come to the wise or wealth to the brilliant or favor to the learned; but time and chance happen to them all. (Ecclesiastes 9:11)

I have fought the good fight; I have finished the race; I have kept the faith. (2 Timothy 4:7)

In the South a hot, humid summer day causes folks to scurry around looking for a cool place. Adults look for resting places, and children seek out playing places. Effie and I had ours. Down under the hill below her house was a favorite place to go. Running through the heavy shade of the hardwood trees was a creek that flowed with a steady stream. Its size changed when the heavy rains came, but even in the midst of a dry summer, the stream kept flowing. Not only was the stream fed by waters from Uncle Tom's pond; it was kept steady by underground springs located all along its way. The stream was always there for us, like the presence of our parents, and we visited often.

Sometimes we pulled off our shoes and socks, rolled up our britches, and waded in the stream's shallow edges, looking for treasures and enjoying its cool touches to our hot feet. Other times we sat on its sandy beaches and dug out holes with our toes. We used our hands to catch and pour its cool waters on our legs and arms. Sometimes we accepted the challenge to catch some of its residents, especially the small minnows that swam in its current. We would turn over rocks that sat in the stream, looking for puppy dog tails or salamanders.

The minnows were seldom caught. They would dart and dodge our attempts to catch with unbelievable speed. Most of the time we lost, but occasionally one of us would cup our hands, dip, and there it was, caught and still swimming in the water we held in our hands. When caught, we would place the minnow in a jar full of water, and unlike with lightning bugs, we did not put holes in the lid or even use one. Minnows can swim but not jump!

We would sit for long spells and watch a minnow swim in the jar. Effie had a tender heart for all earth's good creatures and was teaching me the same. Before leaving the creek we would dump the water and the minnow back in the stream and watch it dart away. It did not hang around to offer thanks for the freedom it had lost and regained.

Our favorite game we played with the creek was boat racing. A roadway through the creek where trucks and tractors made their way either to the fields or back home for lunchtime carved out a deeper place and a clean one from brush and roots. This was our place to play. The game of boat racing needed a more virgin spot. Near the roadway, the creek unchanged by human progress and only slightly modified by the cows crossing the stream, flowed more naturally.

It was this spot upstream that was for boat racing. The stream curved and wove its way, following its natural path to miss trees and to flow around elevated places. Dead branches that had fallen from the trees lay in the stream, causing whatever floated from upstream to dodge and dart or else get stuck. Leaves also fell from the trees and would float freely in the current until they met an obstacle and would stop for a spell or accumulate much like folks at church on the front steps before church began. The creek ran too quietly to hear. It was only at the interrupted places that one could hear the music of the creek. In places where the creek dropped its waters over lower places or was forced through a more narrow space by rocks or grass, its silence gave way to pleasant sounds that Effie and I enjoyed when rest and thought, not play, were better choices.

It was north of the fence where the cows congregated to drink their water that Effie and I went for our boat races. We liked a little more dangerous and exciting place for racing. There were curves and elevations, detours and mazes that forced our boats to use finesse as well as speed.

Effie and I had two boats we raced. One was the leaves that fell from the trees, and the other was the bark that hung loosely on the trunk of some of the trees. There was plenty of both, making our choices more difficult. We would scurry around in the woods looking for large, broad leaves or for long, narrow ones, choosing the ones that we thought would not only float but float with speed. The bark hung from the older trees like dead skin ready to be peeled off. The leaves already had their shapes. The bark we broke and shaped to meet our taste. The more we played our game, the better we built our boats.

"Race time," one of us would call. If Effie wasn't ready, she would plead for more time to shape her boat or find the fastest leaf. "Not ready" was a reason for delay, but never a reason to cancel the game. "Race time," I called again. Effie and I made our way to the starting line. It was an open place where the boats could be launched easily and freely.

It wouldn't be fair to race a bark boat against a leaf boat or a leaf boat against a bark boat. They were too different. We agreed that each race was for a specialized boat.

"Let's race our leaf boat first," said Effie with excitement and anticipation.

"Okay," I said. "Let's go!"

My impatience was fed more by my excitement to race than by my need to win. We both sat steadily on our ankles, bending over the water from opposite banks. Since Effie was older, she always held the starting whistle. Boats in place but not yet free from our grasp, Effie said, "Ready, set, go!" We released our grip and trusted our boats to the stream. We walked along the bank of the creek with a steady pace, keeping up with our swiftly moving boats. Our boats navigated the curves, spun out, and moved in new directions when blocked by a limb or a rock or by a lily pad. At this point our pace slowed, and we hardly moved. We waited for our boats to navigate the hazards and move back out into the open space to pick up speed again. A spectator could easily locate our boats by watching where we stood on the banks of the creek. Effie was out front, moving slowly but still moving. My boat in a locked position, held firmly against a jutting rock by the pressure of the stream, was completely stationary.

The races had few rules. One rule was that stalled, stuck boats could be dislodged by their owners to continue in the race. I reached down and gently pushed my boat free. Soon I was walking again, keeping pace with Effie on the opposite bank. Effie was still out front, but the distance was fast closing. "Come on; come on," I cried, as if my boat by some mysterious remote control was under my direct supervision. Effie's boat floated across the finish line first. I was not upset, hurt, or angry. Just disappointed!

Alternating races between our leaf boats and our bark boats, the races continued until either time was used up or interest exhausted. There were plenty of boats left for future races. The good thing about each race was not winning but finishing. Today, we both finished. We locked our arms around each other as we climbed the red clay hill and left the creek to flow its course and our boats to travel with it.

Rollin' Store

Sharing

Something heard a hundred times is not quite the same as doing it once.

I will make rivers flow on barren heights, and springs within the valleys. I will turn the desert into pools of water, and the parched grounds into springs. (Isaiah 41:18)

Taste and see that the Lord is good. (Psalm 34:8a)

Give and it will be given to you. (Luke 6:38a)

If you can't get the country to the store, get the store to the country. That is called a rollin' store. My first memory of going to the rollin' store was walking down our steps, through the open gate, past the cedar trees to a store that I could hear coming but was not yet in sight. I knew when Mr. Pete revved the motor on his store to leave Aunt Donnie's house it would be only seconds before it would stop right beside our mailbox.

Three things country folks sit on their porches and wait for are yellow buses, mail cars, and rollin' stores. One brought children home from school; one delivered letters, papers, Sears & Roebuck catalogs, and sometimes baby chicks; and the third brought more goodies than a child could want or even imagine. Mr. Pete and his rollin' store came every Wednesday, as predictable as the morning mail.

Rollin' stores, like convenience stores today, were quick fixes for emptying pantries. They brought things Mom needed in between visits to the real store, one that sat on concrete blocks, not rolling wheels! Mama didn't buy much, just what she needed and occasionally something she wanted.

Mom's favorite purchase was a tiny box of some good treat that never made it to the big, brown paper bag but went directly to her hand and into her apron pocket. "I'll take one of those small boxes of peach," she said as soon as Mr. Pete opened the store door. I could not understand why peaches stuffed into a little can made such a treat for my mom. If it were such a treat, why keep it a secret? It was much later that I learned that powdered tobacco with a peach flavor was snuff. Ladies on the hill dipped privately. They made a purchase a well-kept secret, much like a Baptist deacon who circles the Red Dot Store, waiting for an empty store so he can enter and make a private purchase.

If a nickel or dime could be found hiding underneath one of Mom's crocheted dresser cloths, I could get a treat too. Sometimes she would share her change; but she usually saved it, cashing it in for dollar bills that she used for necessities, like loaf bread or a bag of sugar.

Effie never met the rollin' store. It moved right past her house as if it were not there. It did not always stop at mine; but if it failed to stop, it always slowed as if disappointed no one was there. A five-pound bag of flour, a box of peach snuff, a candy bar, or an ice cream sandwich made stopping more frequent than not.

Late one evening as we sat watching the sun go down, I asked, "Effie, does the rollin' store ever stop at your house?"

"I know it goes by, but we don't have any money to make it stop. I've never seen inside a rollin' store. What is it like?"

"A rollin' store is much like a dug-out bus. Instead of seats there are shelves that stretch from ceiling to floor. Each shelf has a narrow guard in front to keep cans and jars from sliding everywhere or crashing to the floor. Each thing has a place, like in church; they sit together in big families. The cans of fruit sit tall and thin. Each has a colored picture drawn tightly around its waist that tells you what has been canned and put inside. The vegetable cans are short and plump, like Aunt Reba and Uncle Tom. Things that come in sacks, like flour and meal, are stacked real straight like stove wood in the early fall. There's sugar for tea cakes, self-rising flour for Mama's biscuits. The corn meal and the grits, shaped differently, lie side by side. Next to the boxes of saltine crackers are flat cans of sardines, Vienna sausage, and potted meat, all of those tasty treats that either sit or lie on top of crackers.

"Close by the scales that hang down from a hook bolted to the ceiling are all those things you buy by the pound. There are bunches of bananas, six or more, with a few singles to make the scales say what you want. All kinds, shapes, and sizes of potatoes lie in bins below, potatoes that you bake, fry, and mash. You point and say what you want, and the store man gets what you say and either puts it on the scales or on the countertop right beside the door. There is not enough room to walk around and get what you want. You have to ask the store man. After weighing what you want, he writes on the side of the brown paper bag what each thing costs. These are things my mom wants.

"Jammed tight against the back of the bus-like store are all the things children are eager to see and to buy. I suspect the location is carefully chosen so children aren't pulling and tugging, begging for a treat as soon as the door opens and they see inside. Just like parents say, 'You have to eat your vegetables before you get any dessert,' even rollin' stores are made for adults first and then children.

"The boxes of Cracker Jacks stand tall and erect, side by side, dressed like soldiers ready for a drill. Crackers shaped like all kinds of animals you can think of are boxed up and held captive, ready to be released so they can run and play before being tasted and eaten. There is a sea of candy that makes you want to jump in and swim, going under and never coming up. There are bars of all kinds: Pay Days; Hershey bars with or without almonds; Snickers, jammed full of nuts; Baby Ruths, named for a great baseball player. There are M&Ms with or without nuts; Sugar Daddies melted on sticks, too hard to chew but great to suck. All flavors of suckers so you have to choose a favorite or get a mixture. Mama likes the chewing gum tray and always gets Juicy Fruit. If I have a penny or two, I get Bazooka; it lasts long and seems to get bigger when chewed.

"My favorite is the ice cream box. It is like a low-cut freezer with room for buckets of ice cream on the bottom that has to be dipped and put in crunchy cones. You have to choose vanilla, chocolate, or strawberry; but if you can't choose, the store man will give you a small dip of each. In the trays that sit up front and slide back and forth so the store man can get to the buckets on the bottom are frozen ice cream treats that you can hold in your hand and eat. Some of my favorites are ice cream sandwiches, vanilla ice cream squeezed between two chocolate cookies; milk sickles, vanilla ice cream frozen on a flat stick covered in melted chocolate that crunches as you bite; fudge sickles that are chocolate ice cream frozen on sticks with no outside cover. In the summer you have to eat in a hurry or you will have to lick on your fingers so as not to waste any good ice cream."

Effie sat there, still, as if she had been captured in a dream. The more I talked, the less she heard. At first she smiled, but then like the sun hiding behind a cloud, her smile disappeared. Her eyes dimmed, and her shoulders drooped. What she heard moved further and further from reality, changing from a dream to a fantasy.

"No, no!" I said. "It's for real! One day I'll show you!"

Disturbed from her dream and with more time on our hands, I could tell she wanted to hear more. Since I was only halfway round the store, I wanted to keep going. My description and her imagination were picking up speed like the water bugs on the still waters of the creek. My description of the store had started at the top of the steps, moving down the right side of the aisle and across the back. I continued, "On the left side of the store are shelves that leave room for the two refrigerated boxes that sit snugly underneath, side by side, to keep things like meat and milk and soft drinks. On most of those shelves are non-eating things, what the store man calls household items. There are scissors, and screwdrivers, packages of needles and spools of thread, bottle openers and pocket knives, black tape and masking tape, lotions and creams, toothpaste and toothbrushes, an entire tray of soaps.

"Next to the driver's seat, close by the store man, as if these things need closer watch, are things not marked but clearly understood for adults. Cigars lie snugly in small wooden boxes, and the cigarettes are stacked in cardboard cartons at least two feet high. The cigars have more regal names like Havana while the cigarettes have more common names like Lucky Strike, Camel, and Kool. For those who prefer homemade cigarettes, hand-rolled, there ars Prince Albert in dressed-up tin cans. If one prefers to chew, there is Bull Durham. The chewing tobacco and the snuff are on the top shelves only in reach of the store man, Mr. Pete. My mom always has change for her box of snuff, and Mr. Pete reaches for it even before she asks. I once found her box and opened it. I did not taste, but I did smell, and it smelled just like its name, peach.

"In the summertime when the heat makes you thirsty, the coolers are a favorite place to shop. Their metal tops slide back and forth, and the trapped cold air rushes out when opened for a purchase. In one cooler is nothing but soft drinks: R.C. or Dr. Pepper, Big Orange Crush, Pepsi, or Coke. If you do not want to have to pay two cents for the bottle, you have to bring back an empty one to buy a full one at regular cost. The drinks are so cold that when the cap is popped, thin slivers of ice float to the top. Sometimes the slivers are so thick you have to shake them down or use the suction of your lips to pry them loose and force them out. A cold soda pop is much like wading into a deep, cold stream. The only difference is that wading starts low and inches up while drinking starts up and inches down."

By the time I made the full round, circling the bus with verbal description, Effie was in disbelief. The rollin' store had become another one of my winged horses, too far, too fast, too much, another fantasy. As the sun lowered and got ready to drop out of sight, bringing on darkness and night, Effie turned and walked away, bathed in a state of sadness and disbelief. It was as if I had offered her something wonderful and then had reached over and taken it back.

Effie and I had begun our visit when the sun was up, and now the sun was down. Somehow that's the way I felt. What was bright light was now darkness. I watched as she limped away, dragging her club foot, slowly disappearing. First her head, then her back, and finally nothing left, not even her foot. She looked as if the added weight in her heart made a more noticeable limp in her walk.

In friendship, what one friend has, the other catches. I was sad because Effie was sad. The sun had set for her and also for me. But why? Why would a rollin' store make me so glad and Effie so sad?

Then, as if God had reversed the sun and brought it back, light dispelling the darkness, I saw and understood. I remembered how I felt when my older brother told me about his visit to see my aunt and uncle who lived near the beach. They took him to the beach to swim in the ocean and to walk on the sandy beach that stretched for miles, holding the ocean in, keeping it from running out and wild. He built sandcastles and rode and jumped waves that broke high and hard near the shore. I was excited at first to hear, but then I started feeling sad. I wondered if I would ever see the ocean and build castles in the sand.

Hearing what my brother had done did not make me want to take it away and somehow make it mine. It made me sad because I thought and felt that his good time would never be mine. Then came the light! Understanding is the first step in the light. Finding a way to make my good time hers was next. Rollin' stores make new stops every week!

I had a full week to make and implement my plan. My plan was simple, but simple does not always mean easy. First, I had to have some money. I had one quarter that I had saved and had tied up in the corner of one of my dad's large white handkerchiefs. I needed one more. One quarter gets you a dream, but two gets you a fantasy!

A nickel or two was possible from my mom who, unlike my dad, thought special, extra tasks were worth some reward. Dad thought tasks came with being born and growing up to be boys and then men. The crocheted dresser cover was the bank inside our house. Any extra change went into the family account. Even though the account was in Mom's name, I could make a withdrawal if I didn't exercise the privilege too often.

The first of the week I checked the account and found a zero balance. Toward the end of the week, the dresser account yielded two nickels.

Almost halfway there with my second quarter. The weekend yielded no additional change, and rollin' store day, Wednesday, was picking up speed like Sambo, our plow horse, when day's work was finished and he was heading home for hay and rest. On Monday morning the account had stabilized. Time and money were speeding in opposite directions.

When need is greater than opportunity, I had learned to turn to the most reliable resource. I knew Mom's coin purse that she kept deep down inside her Sunday pocketbook always housed some loose coins. Dresser cloths were not off-limits, but Mom's coin purse was! I had been to Mom a couple times for school projects, and she had come through. The difference here was I had to sell her the reason for the request. How could I sell her a reason I could not name? I thought of many schemes, sliding through side or back doors. I finally decided to be direct yet to protect my secret.

On Sunday morning I looked and waited for the right time. Mom had finished breakfast. She had made up most of the beds and had sat down to rest in the swing on the north end of the porch. I gave her some time to ease into her rest. I walked almost unnoticed and sat in one of the six rockers that lined the outside wall of the front bedroom. I felt, after a moment, that Mom must have been thinking, "Bobby must want something." She certainly had her reasons to believe that. Sitting with her in a grown-up rocker in midmorning wasn't exactly one of my predictable behaviors. I was tempted to slide in sideways, but my prior plans and my internal hunch said, "Go in straight!"

"Mom," I said, firm and direct. "There is something I want to do that is real special, and I need two quarters. I saved one quarter, and I found two nickels. I need three more."

"What in the world do you need that much money for?" she asked.

My mom sensed my sincere request and treated it seriously even though she said, "Two quarters! That is a lot of money. I'll see." That answer from my mom usually meant delay but seldom no. I was unquestionably assured that my request and my secret were heard and respected. I went to bed, still anxious about my need but less so because my mom was partnering with me in my secretive plan. Two days till rollin' store day!

My lingering anxiety was short-circuited. As I reached over on the chair to retrieve the things I had taken from my pockets the night before to return them to their rightful place, my pockets, I reached deep down into my right pocket to push it to full length. Surprisingly, I felt and counted three nickels. "A miracle," I thought. The miracle was not that my mom gave me the nickels but that she had three nickels to give. I walked into the kitchen. She was standing at the stove. We exchanged glances that confirmed my discovery. Nothing more was ever said. Love in our family was often shared but not often spoken.

Two younger and lots of older brothers cause one to think about where to hide money. To make a deposit in the bank, either in town or in the corner of my underwear drawer, was not an option. Perhaps I could dig a hole beside the pecan tree and bury my silver and my secret. Our dog, Fluffy, always checked out newly dug-up ground. The best way to make sure I could afford my secret was to keep the quarter and five nickels buried deep in my pants pocket. I would keep my pants clean enough so Mom would not rush them to the wash.

The coins never left my pocket and seldom left my hand. When my hand came out for a break, I would check quickly to see if the coins were where they needed to be. As the day moved on toward dinner, then afternoon and early evening, keeping guard over my unprotected treasure became a chore. Yet the burden of the task lightened each time I thought of Effie and the rollin' store.

It was late June. The plum bushes had dressed themselves with red and yellow balls that looked like marbles of all sizes. Some were small, but others looked like log rollers, oversized marbles that were mixed in with a package of marbles that we got for Christmas or birthdays. I planned it so we could pick plums next to the road where the rollin' store runs.

With milk bucket in hand, I skipped down the road with the change jingling in my pockets, more excited than when one picks plums. Effie was in her room playing with her doll. The door was standing wide open, and the wooden windows had been let down, reminding me of children on the school playground when they hooked their feet on the bar and hung upside down.

"Effie," I said, in a low, calm voice, making sure my plan was inside my head. "Let's go up by the road and pick plums. Mama wants to make some jelly." Effie, being the older and the bigger of the two, had to reestablish her control with every invitation initiated by me by deliberating her decision. Then she moved like the wind on a still day. That was fine with me. A plan is a good plan when it works, no matter how it moves on to the end.

The plum bushes were so gracious with their plums. Each year as predictable as summer itself, the bushes would decorate themselves with their goodies colored in bright reds and golden yellows. The only problem was the competition we had with the birds, squirrels, and green crawling worms. They liked plums too! Most summers there were enough plums for all of us.

The buckets were filling up fast when my ears picked up the sound of the rollin' store. I wove my way in and out through the thick plum bushes and stood on the side of the road in clear sight. I waved my arms like a road man does when the road has been washed out by heavy rains. Rollin' store drivers look for waving arms or folks just standing by the road. A waving customer is the best friend a rollin' store man has.

The driver's foot came off the gas and rested lightly and soon more firmly on the brakes. I knew I had been seen. "Effie, come on," I cried. Effie stood there in surprise. Frozen by her disbelief, she moved forward not one inch. "Come on," I cried again. "He won't stop long!" Her disbelief, like a block of ice in the shade, melted slowly. The rollin' store slowed down to a trot, then a fast walk, and finally to a dead halt. Effie, unlike the store, had picked up her pace and was standing beside me on the road. I reached down in my pocket and felt the joy of my secret. I retrieved the quarter and five nickels, holding them tightly in my hand, much like when I caught my first lightning bug.

When the door opened wide, Effie and I stood side by side. I reached over and pulled her by the arm and opened my hand wide, and she just stood there. I said, "This is yours. Buy what you want!" Still hesitant, I reached and got her hand. She opened it, and I laid in her hand both my treasure and my secret.

I waited for her to step into the store ahead of me. She made a quick survey of the store, remembering my recent detailed description. After her survey Effie moved quickly. To my surprise Effie's purchases were quickly made, and we stepped outside the door. The store man thanked us for shopping, closed the door, and moved on his way. Effie and I walked away from the road. She carried a small brown paper bag, rolled halfway down, tightly between her thumb and pointin' finger. We sat down on the bank of the road that ran by her house in the shade of a half-grown water oak. She slowly unfurled her paper bag and lifted out her big Orange Crush. Reaching in the second time, she fetched out a box of animal crackers. That was no surprise to me, knowing how much Effie loved animals.

Looking in her box of animal cookies, Effie did something that did not surprise me. She offered me the open box to choose a cookie. I chose a lion. Its hump on its back meant more cookie for me! Then Effie did surprise me. She spread out the hanging part of her dress and placed each animal cookie one by one, side by side, on her dress. She studied each one, picked each one up and held it for a moment, then placed it back on her dress. She kept the monkey in her hand. It was the first to be selected for her late-morning snack. She unscrewed the cap on her orange Crush and ate and drank while I ate.

Reaching back into her paper bag, Effie retrieved five pieces of Bazooka bubblegum and held out her hand for me to choose one. Together, we unwrapped the pieces of bubblegum, read the cartoon that came with it, and began chewing a treat that lasted forever. We started blowing bubbles. Soon we were in a contest to see which one could blow the biggest one, having to use the chewed gum in our mouths to grab off the gum on our lips and nose from our busted bubbles.

I never asked Effie about her choices. Somehow when you have to give an account, it changes a gift into an obligation. I didn't ask about the change left over either. I just knew that the rollin' store would stop again at her place.

As the days passed, Effie and I talked often about the rollin' store. One thing was different. A descriptive report had been transformed into a shared experience.

Cane Syrup and Pumlins

New Life

A pumlin is a stalk of sugar cane with the life squeezed out of it.

I tell you the truth, unless a kernel of wheat falls to the ground and dies, it remains only a single seed. But if it dies, it produces many seeds. (John 12:24)

Listen, I tell you a mystery: we will not all sleep, but we will all be changed—in a flash, in the twinkling of an eye, at the last trumpet. For the trumpet will sound, the dead will be raised, and we will be changed. (1Corinthians 15:51–52)

Two creeks flowed from the west, moving east through a bottom of land that lay flat against the woods in front of our house. One of the creeks flowed into a six-acre pond that my dad and brothers had built for fishing and swimming. The creek that delivered water to the pond and kept it filled and well supplied gave much and kept little. It flowed steady along its carved-out path until it met the pond, slowed down, and continued along its way with the overflow water that the pond did not need or keep.

The other creek flowed slightly north of its companion. Its water was steady and its stream unchanged except by the weather or by some fallen tree that fell across its path or by a den of beavers who worked hard to divert its course with a highly engineered dam of their own that created deeper waters for the beavers' plans. Eventually, the pushing pressure of the moving stream would quickly or slowly dislodge the blockage and return the stream to its steady flow.

Effie and I claimed the creeks as frequent sources for cooling pleasures and as stages for first-class entertainment. They gave us cool waters for our dusty feet and cool breezes to revive us on hot, humid days. They gave us water bugs that danced on their waters and darting minnows that played hide and seek in the rocks and shadows of their streams. Red birds bathed in their waters, and cows drank from their unlimited supply. Minnows fed from their tables and quickly grew to be the fish we caught, cleaned, and ate from our tables.

The added moisture from their banks watered the soil to grow the cane groves that provided us our fishing poles and pop guns. Huckleberries grew by their side, and dogwoods dotted the woods with white and pink blossoms. Sassafras roots were dug from their sides and boiled to make our houses smell good and to fill our cups with tea. The trees that grew tall and wide formed an archway through which we often walked and played.

They were giving creeks. It seemed that the more they got, the more they shared. They were fed by smaller streams that joined them along the way. When it rained hard or long, they carried the extra water. The creeks were like natural irrigation systems, giving water freely so the trees and plants could live long and fruitful lives.

There were some things my dad grew just for us; there were other things that he planted to share with neighbors and friends. He planted corn and peas, one field after another, staggering their planting so we could have fresh vegetables all summer and into early and middle fall. The corn we did not eat was harvested and stored to feed the hogs and cows through the winter months and on into spring. Farming for my dad was like going to school. What one learned in a lower grade was carried forward to the next year and a higher grade. Dad planted corn for this season and the next.

The sugar cane patch was planted every year. It was a patch that supplied syrup for all our neighbors. Sugar cane planted by the creek was as predictable as Mama's pregnancies. In visiting with our neighbors, I always knew that there was an unspoken expectation that come late fall, there would be a new supply of cane syrup. Cane syrup was treated as a necessity and not an extra in everyone's pantry. For every child, whether black or white, syrup was the favorite and most frequent dessert: hot biscuits, fresh butter, and thick, drippy cane syrup. Even though it was my dad's patch, it was the neighbors' syrup!

Children liked not only the syrup; we liked to slide on the pumlins that were thrown in the great gulley behind the cane mill. Pumlins are the cane stalks after all the juice has been squeezed out. Piled together, they make a soft, slick slide.

Effie and I liked to watch a lot and help a little with the sugar cane and the syrup-making. After each year's fall cutting, Dad would put enough of the cane stalks aside to make sure the syrup-making kept going year after year after year. The cane stalks that he sorted out of the cane cutting were the very best stalks. They were the ones he would use for seeding the following year. He graded those stalks out as "A" stalks.

The selected stalks were neatly stacked on a low-bodied wagon and hauled up to the house. Ease and my brothers would dig long, deep trenches, covering them with freshly raked pine straw. God must have known what was required for making syrup, because everything needed was close by—the pine trees, the creek, and the dark, good soil.

After each of the trenches was lined with ample amounts of fresh pine straw, the stalks of sugar cane were carefully laid into the cushioned beds. The stalks were covered with thick straw, and scoops of gray, sandy dirt were thrown on top, making the mounds of dirt look like the unmarked graves at the church. Ease would observe the finished work and say, "Well, we have put the cane to rest. Come summer, there will be a mighty resurrection!"

I always wanted to know more about resurrection because my grandpa had died right after I was born, and I kept hearing my mama say when we made our yearly visit to the church cemetery for cleaning-off day, "Grandpa and Grandma are buried here, right here. They are resting now. When Jesus comes, they will rise up and be resurrected." Resurrection was a big word for me. I really didn't understand, but I was beginning to.

Each spring, when all that looked so dead began to rise, Effie would talk to me about God. All the trees that had undressed in the fall and stood stark naked in the winter would put on a new green outfit and stand with pride, fully dressed as if ready to go to church and sing the songs of faith and celebration. There was a pear tree, snarled and old, that stood between Effie's house and mine. Each winter, the pear tree looked dead. Hope dimmed for one of those large, golden pears that tasted so firm and sweet. In spring Effie would point to the pear tree and say, "Look, Bobby. See God's miracle." The old pear tree that looked so dead had every sign of life.

First there were the new green shoots. Next, the tiny leaves, tender and green, would slowly unfold and fit each branch with long, green gloves. Tiny white blossoms would show and mix with the green leaves to make a flower arrangement too big for the table at church but just right for the field where Dad planted his fruit tree that he had ordered straight out of the Sears & Roebuck catalog. "When a tree looks dead," Effie would say, "God is working out of sight. You have to wait 'til spring to know what God's been doing."

Effie loved her flowers. Her favorite was the bright yellow daffodil. Each time I walked down to her house in the early spring, Effie would take me over to the corner of her yard where she would point to a place in her flower bed and say, "It's coming." I would look long and hard and see nothing. I thought Effie had better eyes than I did or that there was a secret to her bed that she knew and I didn't. There was! I had to wait to see it for myself.

On a return trip I began to see what Effie saw. The bulbs she had planted years before, which slept through the long days and nights of winter, in the spring opened their eyes, stretched their arms, squeezed their silky brown bodies, and pushed a plant that seemed to whisper quietly each spring, "Good morning. It's good to see you again." Soon, a tightly woven bloom would appear and sit there patiently on a long, thin stem. Taking its time, basking in the warmth of the sun, breathing in the fresh air of spring, the bloom would open its tightly closed lips and sing its song of spring.

Effie was careful with her corner bed. Some of the yellow-throated daffodils she would cut and share with Panella to bring some of newly born spring into the darkness of her lingering winter. Some of her flowers she would cut and stand them in a fruit jar half filled with water and walk them up to my house for Miss Lula. She kept enough to add color to the corner of her bed. "God brings lots of his heaven down to earth," Effie would quietly say. "Some God keeps for himself."

Effie and I liked to help Ease plant the sugar cane. Early one morning Ease had gotten up, dressed, eaten several biscuits filled with white fatback bacon, harnessed Molly the mule, and was already plowing the deep furrows in the cane patch before Effie and I got there. Ease plowed so slowly that when he let us hold the plow, we could easily keep up. Most grown folks walk like grown folks, too fast for small children. Effie was older and bigger, but she had to walk with her club foot. Ease walked just right for us even though he was a grown folk. Walking slow was something Ease did best. Molly insisted on walking like a grown folk. Ease would pull hard on the reigns to slow her down.

The freshly plowed dirt was cool and soft to our early spring feet. The plow sliced through the ground, cutting a deep furrow and piling up the dirt on both sides. Sometimes we would snag a root and the plow would pop forward and up. Ease would stop Molly, reset the plow, and we would keep plowing.

As Ease plowed back and forth, back and forth, the cane patch began to look like Effie's head after Queen had plaited her hair. The furrows were straight and narrow and went from one end of the field to the other. When all the furrows had been plowed, Ease unhitched Molly from the plow and rode her to the house. Effie and I walked close behind. It was time to uncover the sleeping cane snuggled down underneath the elevated mounds of dirt, wrapped in warm blankets of pine straw.

The wagon had been left near the sleeping cane stalks that had been lying undisturbed since last fall. Ease took a scoop and lifted off each mound of dirt. Effie and I dug out any remaining dirt and then lifted the blankets of pine straw to see the purple stalks of sugar cane, each lying on top of the other, peacefully sleeping. It must have been a shock to their eyes to look up into the light after sleeping in the dark for so long. Eyes used to the dark take a while to adjust to the light.

It was fun to dig beneath the mounds, to lift the straw and see the stalks of sugar cane. I felt both friend and foe. We were friend to have a part in their resurrection and foe to disturb their long winter sleep. Effie and I helped Ease load the wagon with as much sugar cane as Molly could pull with the added weight of Effie and me sitting on the back of the wagon, dangling our legs and feet in the air.

The wagon trip down to the creek was slow and bumpy. I felt some guilt. Molly worked and pulled so hard. We rode in such ease! Ease pulled Molly up on the edge of the field next to where all the furrows lay open, ready for the cane. Each one of us lifted off the wagon as many stalks as we could carry and laid them one by one, end to end, into the furrows. When we finished, the furrows looked like an open graveyard with rows and rows of the same-size bodies lying head to feet, ready to be covered, waiting for a "mighty resurrection."

Effie and I got tired before Ease. While he and Molly plowed the loose dirt on both sides back into the open furrows, covering the sugar cane with warm, loose dirt, we sat and rested under the great big water oak that had massive arms and a thick trunk bigger than Cousin Chickey.

When Ease and Molly moved away from us toward the other end of the row, there was a silence much like silent prayer time in church. The only sounds were the chirping of the birds and the flowing sound of the creek. Any sound from the creek was an invitation to come again and explore her gifts. Soon Effie and I were walking by her side, playing hide and seek with the minnows that swam unnoticed in her shallow waters. Scared by our unexpected presence, the minnows would scurry off into deeper waters where shadows kept them safe, hidden from our presence.

Slowly, when fear was no longer needed, the minnows would return to the shallow waters.

Refreshed by our visit to the creek, we walked back to the field where Ease and Molly were still plowing, throwing the dirt back into the furrows from both sides. Some rows of cane bodies were still uncovered, but others lay resting underneath the blankets of warm, dry dirt. We stayed around until all the cane bodies were covered, reminding me of death, not life. Effie reassured me, as she often did, that things that die in God's own plan live again.

Several weeks passed, and I had completely forgotten about the cane patch. Effie hadn't! "Let's walk over to the creek by the cane patch. Daddy told me it was coming up." It was a bright, sunny day. Spring was fast fading, and summer was picking up speed. The ground was warm to our feet. A breeze, strong enough to cause the growing grass to give a friendly wave, kept the sweat from forming on our faces. "Look!" cried Effie in a shrieking voice that I only heard when she was surprised by something new or unexpected. Down each of the mounded furrows there were hundreds, thousands, of tiny, thin green shoots peeping up from under the covers of the earth. Gazing out over the cane patch, it looked like someone had come in overnight and laid a bright green carpet. "Look at the resurrections," I exclaimed as we ran back and forth over and between the furrows, making sure we did not step on even one of God's new creations.

The creek supplied the water, except for the summer showers that weren't predicted but came often enough to partner with the creek. The fertile soil gave plenty of food. The hot sun rose earlier and stayed longer, helping to pull the growth up and out. After a few weeks the new shoots were tall as my knees and had multiple arms hanging by their sides. The shoots slowly turned into stalks that grew bigger and taller. Soon they reached my eyes and then my head.

Toward the end of summer, each stalk was taller than anyone we knew. Their arms had grown longer and drooped more closely by their sides. The stalks began to change color from pale green to darker green to purplish green. The purple in the stalk gave evidence that fall and harvest were approaching, time to clean the kettle and check out the grinder. Dad was consulting with Ease about the best days for cooking. Once syrup started cooking, it had to go on, even through the night and into the next day. Syrup-cooking days were decided, and that meant time to strip and cut the cane.

The cane mill was up the road and around the corner, at Uncle Ed's and Aunt Mabel's house. Aunt Mabel was my daddy's sister, and our milk cow was named for her. She and Daddy were not close except for two times each year. One was when Aunt Mabel, Aunt Donnie, and Mama baked Christmas cakes. The other was at syrup-cooking time.

Uncle Ed was a good mechanic. He had the cane grinder fixed, oiled, and ready to go. Ease had cut several loads of cane, had hauled them around to the cane mill, and had stacked the cane in a tall, wide pile near the grinder. Molly was hitched to a long pole that was attached to the grinder and to Molly's harness. She moved in an endless circle that let her go and yet not go anywhere. Her footsteps were all the same because she could not vary her path even if she tried. And sometimes Molly would. That was her temperament. At the cane mill her strength was used and her rebellion controlled.

Molly's circling reminded me of what my dad would say sometimes: "Son, you go 'round and 'round in circles. That won't get you anywhere!" Molly worked hard, and one of my older brothers would stop her occasionally to either let her rest or to give her some water or some part of the dried bale of peanut hay that Dad kept against the grinder.

One of my older cousins or one of my older brothers would feed the cane into the grinder, and it would take all it could get, eating one stalk at the time. It would take the cane into its open mouth, bite down between two sets of steel teeth, chew hard and long until all the juice was out and drained into a funnel that channeled the juice flow into a five-gallon bucket. As the buckets would fill with fresh cane juice, one bucket would be replaced by another while the juice was poured into a wooden barrel. The pumlins were piled on the ground, and when the pile reached a certain height, they would be pitchforked into a deep gulley that was a short distance from the cane mill. The gulley was separated from the cane mill by a barbed-wire fence to keep the cows from scaring Molly or chewing some of the cane for themselves.

When the barrel was full, two strong men carried it over to the large black kettle. It took five barrels of the cane juice to make a cooking. The kettle sat on four brick pillars, raising it so its drooping stomach would hang near the ground but high enough to build a fire underneath the sagging stomach of the kettle. Dad would load his truck with kindling to get the fire started and firewood of oak and hickory to keep the fire going. With plenty of both from trees on the farm, Dad never ran out of wood.

Ease kept a long-handled metal dipper in his hand, stirring the boiling sugar cane juice and dipping off any foam or trash that floated to the top. Occasionally, a camel fly or a buzzing yellow jacket, attracted by the sweet smell of the syrup cooking in the kettle, would lite or dive into the boiling juice. Under the watchful eye of Ease, it would be dipped out, too late to save its life but fast enough to keep it from adding any foreign substance to the syrup.

While the adults worked, keeping watch over the fire and the bubbling kettle, the children would play. Hide and seek was a favorite game but at the cane mill the most popular game was pumlin sliding. After the juice was squeezed out of the stalk of cane, the remains would fall to the ground lifeless. They would collect, piling on each other, creating a pumlin mountain. Molly liked for it to grow tall because she would get to rest while one of Uncle Ed's boys took them over to the gulley and dump them. The side of the gully nearest the sugar cane mill was carved out like a great big playground slide. The pumlins, when dumped, would slide down the side of the gully, each one trying to slide further than the other. If the pumlins could play, so could the children.

Since syrup-cooking time was always announced in advance, Effie and I would keep our eyes open for large cardboard boxes. The big, sturdy boxes that brought all kinds of things to my daddy's store—canned vegetables, work shoes, premium crackers—were perfect slides when carefully disassembled. Effie and I had the best slides ever! Daddy surprised Mama. He saved some money from the sale of his peanuts and bought Mama a brand-new white enamel stove. I stored the large box that housed the stove in one of the walk-in closets. When it was time to slide, Effie and I used Daddy's wire cutters to cut loose the sides of the box to make four awesome slides. We had enough slides for all of us to play.

In late fall the night was cold. It made the fire feel warm, the syrup-cooking smell wonderful, and the cane juice cold. There was no limit to how much juice we drank! You can't want too much cane juice because it is so sweet! One of Aunt Mabel's small jars was always available.

After playing a game of hide and seek, Effie and I went to the wagon and got our cardboard slides. The pumlin slide was covered well and, like a new bed of snow, untouched. The night was cold and clear, and the moon was full. The moonlight reflected off the pumlins, giving them a clear, slick shine. "Watch out!" said one of my older brothers. "It's going to be fast." Effie was older and more careful and cautious. She went first only when there was no danger. I was too young to be afraid of anything that looked like fun. I laid my slide on the brown grass that grew to the edge of the gully. It was dry and thick and held the slide in place until it was time to ride.

A crowd of folks had gathered to watch the first slide of the year. That raised my excitement and lowered my fear. The crowd was there, ready for someone to christen the brand new pumlin slide. My new cardboard slide was unmarked, waiting to be used. I pulled my flannel shirt tight across my chest and laid my slide on the grass. I could feel the excitement and the fear all mixed in together. It was a special moment for me, and I was determined not to let the fear rob me of my excitement nor my special appearance before the crowd. I remember what my dad had said to me when I stood on our diving board at the pond for the first time: "Don't stand there holding on to your fear. It will get bigger. Go ahead and jump."

The mixture of fear and excitement rose up in me and then overflowed, like foam does when you shake a bottled coke. I slid my slide forward, laid most of my body on the sled, extended both legs straight up, pulled the two sides toward the middle, and pushed off. The first time was too quick to think about where I was or how I was doing. In seconds I was at the bottom, and the first sounds I heard were clapping and then screaming, "Way to go, Bobby! Great ride!" The crowd disappeared. The adults had come to make syrup, not judge pumlin slides.

I sat at the bottom for a while, motioned for Effie to come, and waited for her to make her first run of the new season. As usual, Effie hesitated. She mounted her new cardboard box slide, pushed off, and made a clean, fast slide, joining me at the foot of the slide. Those were the first two of many more slides as we played our game while Ease stirred and skimmed off the syrup.

We mixed our games of sliding and hiding and added a third one that flirted with an unexpected danger. Hiding underneath the pumlins was our third and newest game. When the pumlins were forked into the gully, some would fall off the fork and build up a collection on the grass near the gully. As the cane juice flowed, the pumlins collected. There were enough at the top of the gully, inside the barbed-wire fence that allowed Aunt Mabel's cows to graze but not roam, to cover Effie and me with soft, freshly squeezed pumlins. Earlier, I had hidden Effie, and now it was her turn to hide me. Effie chose a safe place, back from the edge of the gully, close to the growing pile of drying pumlins.

This burial was going to be the best burial ever! We got one of Uncle Ed's long-handle scoops and dug out a hole deep enough for me to lie half down with my head even with the top of the hole. My legs were stretched out and my arms close to my body. We laid a thick layer of the driest pumlins in the hole to cover the damp dirt, making the grave soft and dry. We lined the sides with dried, squeezed-out stalks. I got in, and Effie asked, "Are you in and ready?" I nodded, giving her the go-ahead. The moon was clear and the light plenty bright for her to see my nod of approval.

The burial was slow and easy. Effie chose only the best pumlins, gently laying them over my chest. Each one was longer than me. It took only a few of them for me to slowly begin to disappear. The moon had risen, and through the thin layer of pumlins, I could see the man I had visited in my fantasy. Once Effie started something, she worked straight through until it was finished. The light from the moon grew dimmer and dimmer until I was buried in utter darkness.

All was quiet. There was no sound of Effie. I decided that she had either gone to relieve herself or she was drinking cane juice out of Aunt Mabel's fruit jar. As I lay still in my freshly dug grave, I thought of Grandpa and Grandma lying there in the graveyard at the church. Only they were dead, and I was still alive!

Suddenly, my calm changed to fear. I could sense something was close by not yet seen or heard. I heard the faint sound of one of Uncle Ed's cowbells. All his cows wore cowbells. Now I knew. The cows were coming my way. Do I sit up or lie still? Do I scream for Effie? Do I scare the cows, causing them to stampede, or do I trust them to know where holes are dug and little boys are buried? I chose to lie perfectly still and silently pray. My preacher always sold prayer as the best remedy for bad times. I chose stillness, not because that was the wise thing to do. Wisdom had not quieted my voice; fear had stolen it!

The quieter I lay, the louder the bells. The only thing I heard inside the grave was my breathing. The only sound I heard outside my hiding place was a medley of bells, not playing any notes but getting louder and louder. Even to a little boy, that meant closer and closer. I breathed faster. My body was as stiff as concrete on my mom's porch. Lying stiff and still, I waited for death. Then something happened. The same fear that had kept me from moving moved me. I sat up like a jack-in-a-box, throwing cane pumlins in all directions. Uncle Ed's cows flushed like a covey of doves when Ole Jack quit pointing and went to catching. They scattered like frightened sheep without a shepherd. Their bells rang loud and clear and then faded as they moved away from the fence and into the woods.

Effie stood silently at first, and then she broke into a laughter I had not heard before. Getting free from her laughter, Effie exclaimed, "Bobby, you done got resurrected 'fore Jesus comes!" When we both settled down, we sat on the edge of my grave looking at each other. The fear broke through the laughter, and both of us knew that we had sat very close to danger.

As we rode home with my daddy in the cab of his truck, there was total silence. Effie was thinking of the cows. I was thinking, "I bet Grandma and Grandpa will be glad when Jesus comes!"

Hellover, Hellover, Send the Ball Over

Chosen

Being chosen last to a child is only slightly better than not being chosen at all.

A man of many companions may come to ruin, but there is a friend who sticks closer than a brother. (Proverbs 18:24)

I have called you friends, for everything that I learned from my Father I have made known to you. You did not choose me but I chose you. (John 15:15–16a)

Not everyone wanted to play baseball. There was no one who did not want to play "hellover, hellover, send the ball over!" Effie, despite her limp, liked to play games with us even though she was usually chosen last.

"Hellover, hellover, send the ball over" was played anytime and anywhere. Late afternoon at my house was best. The chores were done, baths were delayed, and the slowly dropping sun seemed to be our friend, lingering as long as it could. It seemed hesitant to go, knowing we needed its light to see the ball crest the top of the house, roll down the steep, sloping roof, gaining speed as it descended, bouncing on the ground. At first we could see the ball clearly. As dusk gave way to dark, we played more by sound than by sight.

There was one part of this game I hated. Two persons, usually the oldest and the biggest, were self-appointed captains. They chose the teams. Alternating turns, they chose us one by one until all were chosen. I was young but fast. I had learned early to catch a ball, so I was chosen not first but near the middle. Never last! But Effie, because she ran carrying her limp, was always the last one chosen. It seemed to hurt me more than her. When she was chosen seemed not nearly as important to Effie as being chosen. She was always last but never left out!

Each team was equal in number and, if the captains could manage it, in skill. Which team started in the back of the house was no debated deal. One captain would volunteer to go to the back, and the other team would be led to the front. Who had the ball first was a hotly debated issue. There were valuable minutes of daylight play wasted by argument over who got the ball first.

"You won last time," one would say.

"I know, but last time we played, you got the ball first."

J. T., one of the captains who was big, loud, and wanted to win far more than he wanted to play, said with authority, "Last time we played, I threw the ball over first. It's your time to throw to us." The game was much like baseball. It was better to have possession last, not first. "Plus," said J. T., as a way to win the argument, "I have Effie on my side." I wish they could have decided without using Effie. But they didn't!

Effie had learned to hide her hurt over being chosen last and being labeled as a detriment to the team. She tried hard not to show it. She didn't cry or even shed a tear. She just stood off to the side and looked away. I wanted to go and stand beside her as a way to unload some of the hurt off her and on to me. But I was on the other team. Loyalty to my team won out over loyalty to my friend. We could talk about it later, but not now. So I stayed with my team. I watched as Effie stood with her team when chosen, apart and alone.

"Let's play," said Della, the captain of my team. We walked to the back side of the house. J. T. and his team walked to the front. Effie walked with them but several steps behind. It was partially because of her foot, but mostly it was the hurt from being chosen last.

"Hellover, hellover, send the ball over" was a favorite game because everybody could play, girl or boy, black or white, small or large, fast or slow. It was like hide and seek. After the two teams were chosen and each team was located, a rubber ball was thrown on top of the house hard and far enough to roll over to the other side. If the throw did not succeed, it would be thrown again. If the throw was a success, the other team would see it coming, and someone on the team had to catch the ball off the house either on a fly or on a one-time bounce. Once the ball was caught, the person with the ball would choose which way to go. The team would go left or right, hoping to surprise the other team and either hit or touch a player on the other team, and that player or players would be captured. Each team tried to capture all the players from the other team.

Seldom were all players captured. If they were all captured, the game was over, new sides were chosen, and a new game began. When time was called or darkness came, usually the team that won was the team with the most players. Each team tried to capture the fastest, best players. Next, the younger, slower players were targeted. I was young but fast enough to be wanted. Effie was slow enough not to be wanted until the very end. This never kept her from running and seeking cover on the other side of the house. When the game began, Effie's hurt seemed to quickly fade away, and Effie would be screaming and laughing like the rest of us.

Della was older, game wise, and fast. Most of us played for fun. Della played to win! She and J. T. were about the same age, possessed equal skills, and competed like warriors.

Della checked her team one by one, then cried "Ready" so all could hear but not loud enough to alert the other team. She caught the ball firmly in her hand, squeezing it with her three middle fingers. She drew her arm up from her side, raised it above her head, and let the ball take flight. It bounced halfway up the roof and rolled back down. She heaved the ball a second time, and it rolled near the top of the roof and again rolled back down. She caught the ball on first bounce and the third time gave it a strong heave, and the ball bounced on the roof and fell over to the other side.

J. T. caught the ball on the fly, and his team was told which direction by a silent finger point. One of our players cried out "Smokehouse, smokehouse," indicating that J. T. and his team would be coming around the east side of the house. The game continued back and forth, back and forth. Neither J. T. nor Della, the two targeted players, was captured. Others of us moved from side to side as we were hit and captured. Finally, darkness and bath calls interrupted the game, and we each left the yard knowing another game was soon to come. J. T. and Della remembered who was on their team. The next game would continue their fierce competition.

Late one afternoon, when a smaller crowd was hanging around trying to decide what to play, Knocker said, "Let's play hellover." Knocker, lean and thin, played games sometimes but not often. He was usually doing something with a tractor or truck. He was so good with plowing and driving that he was treated more like an adult than a boy. A few grumbled aloud, "Let's play something else," but most wanted to please Knocker. Soon, we had formed a circle around Knocker, knowing that he was in charge.

"Let's choose teams," he said. Everyone began to scream, "Let me choose! Let me choose! I've never been a chooser. Let me choose!" Knocker let it go for a while. Then, like Moses, he raised both hands and shouted, "Hush. Listen up."

Knocker was a different soul. He never fit anything or anywhere. It wasn't that he wanted to be different or tried to be different; he just *was* different. When we walked to the pond, we followed the road tracks made by the trucks and tractors. Not Knocker! We never knew which way he would go. He might use the road down by Ease's house or through the woods by Uncle Tom's or follow the trails made by the cows. He chose his own path to the pond.

"Ellie Mae, you be one of the choosers today." Ellie Mae was younger than Knocker but older than I. She was a fast runner but not a good catcher. She had never been a captain before. As soon as she was chosen, the cries began again. This time they were stronger and louder. Those who had never been a chooser and who never expected to be one were yelling, waving their hands as tall as they could and pushing in toward Knocker. He let it go for a shorter period of time. Hands up, clamoring ceased, and Knocker came out with a life-altering surprise: "Bobby, you be the other chooser." I couldn't believe it! I was smaller and could hardly be seen or heard. But Knocker was different!

Ellie Mae stood to one side, and I stood to the other. She was older, taller, and better than I was, and Knocker knew that. He quickly turned and said to me, "Bobby, you choose first." The yelling stopped, and everyone stood looking at me. I was little, but I was in charge. I had never felt so big in my life. Who should I choose? Did Knocker expect me to choose him? He had chosen me. Most everyone waited, knowing I would choose either J. T. or Della. They were the biggest, the fastest, and the best. If I chose J. T., Ellie Mae would choose Della. If I chose Della, Ellie Mae would choose J. T. That was expected. Either way, our teams would start off about even.

As I stood there, I was holding some things everyone knew and something nobody knew but me. Everyone knew I was a chooser. They knew I would pick the best ones for the team, and we all knew who they were. They knew I would pick Effie last. What no one knew was that I had had a dream several nights before. In the dream I was one of the pickers, and my first pick was Effie.

What do I do? Do I go with what they expect, or do I go with what I dreamed? Knocker had given me a gift that I always longed for and wanted, but now that I had it, I wished he had given it to someone else. J. T. was so good. If I chose him, my team would probably win. If I didn't, we would probably lose. I was little and young, and I wanted to win. I was about to go with my need to win and my desire to be admired and accepted when out of the corner of my eye I saw a red bird sitting on one of the electric wires that ran from the tall, black pole down by the road to the side of our house. I saw Effie standing over to the side, looking away. Choosing was so painful for her. She waited for everyone to be chosen.

She would walk to the side of the one who had last pick. Most of the time her name was not even called!

"Effie," I said, breaking the silence. Suddenly, what had been a dream was now a reality. The crowd sneered and shook their heads. They couldn't believe it! "Dumb head!" they said. Ellie Mae chose J. T., and I chose Della. We walked to the front, and they walked to the back. The game was played as usual, and soon no one remembered that I had chosen Effie.

I went to bed thinking to myself, "A dream sure is easier than choosing." Yet I drifted off to sleep with a grin on my face, a warm smile in my heart, and a red bird on my mind.

A Special Kerchief

Self-Worth

There are those special times when extravagance is the only expression of love.

While Jesus was in Bethany in the home of a man known as Simon the Leper, a woman came to him with an alabaster jar of very expensive perfume, which she poured on his head as he was reclining at the table.

When the disciples saw this, they were indignant. "Why this waste?" they asked. "This perfume could have been sold at a high price and the money given to the poor."

Aware of this, Jesus said to them, "Why are you bothering this woman? She has done a beautiful thing to me. The poor you will always have with you, but you will not always have me. When she poured this perfume on my body, she did it to prepare me for burial. I tell you the truth, wherever this gospel is preached throughout the world, what she has done will also be told, in memory of her." (Matthew 26:6–13)

Effie was often without her shoes, sometimes without her hat, but seldom without her handkerchief. It was part of who she was, just like her arm or her club foot.

Most of her handkerchiefs were not store-bought. They were parts of feed and flour sacks that Effie, with permission from Panella, cut away. Effie kept her eye on the sack in the barn, checking often to see when it would be hers to cut and wash, making a head scarf, a bandanna, or one of her many kerchiefs.

In summer Effie carried with her a bead of sweat that sat snugly on her upper lip. The beads of sweat collected on her broad, firm lip and sat there like drops of early-morning dew on the leaf of one of Mom's elephant ears. As soon as she wiped some of the beads away, others appeared. Out would come her kerchief, and in one quick stroke they were wiped away and gone. Her lip was dry and clean, like the coffee table in our living room that had been dusted and polished with Johnson's clean-all wax.

Effie did have a few store-bought kerchiefs—not nearly as many as the ones cut from the feed and flour sacks, but she had more than one. They were used only for special occasions. There was one that was soft, airy, and bordered with lace. In the corner sat a bouquet of pink and blue flowers. The kerchief was never stored away in her pocket, but she carried it in her hand. Occasionally, it was used to dry her sweat-beaded lip. This kerchief was not a dusting rag. It was a fancy blotter. She would unfold it from her protective clutch and carefully fold it over twice. She would lift it to her lip, press gently, and the beads of sweat disappeared from her lip like spilled milk underneath one of Mom's fluffy towels. Her kerchief would rest safely in her folded hand until another collection of beads required that she unfold it again, and the entire process would repeat itself with unbelievable predictability.

Her favorite kerchief was the one that held money for a "surcie." For Effie a surcie was a special favor you gave to yourself because occasionally you needed or wanted one.

Effie earned money in a variety of ways. She lived at home with older sisters who had children, and she would babysit. Miss Lula, my mama, would surprise Effie with a nickel or dime when she brought her a bouquet of gardenias that grew on her large bush in the far corner of her yard; or a fruit jarful of jonquils with tall, spindly stems; or some purple wild violets she had picked by the creek. Occasionally, the sister who had moved north and who sent her presents at Christmas would send her a dollar bill. She would get it changed at the store into nickels, dimes, and quarters so she could tie them in the corner of her kerchief.

Sometimes Effie would add her money to the money Ease made by working on the farm, and she would walk to the store, two miles away, to buy groceries for her mom. Grocery money she carried in her handheld purse that snapped so tightly she would have to work to pry it open. Sugar for syrup cakes, potatoes to boil or to fry, salted fish, a cut of cheese, Effie carried the order in her head and purchased exactly what she had been sent to the store to get. Groceries bagged, she would clutch the bags in her arms, making sure the bags did not tear and the groceries did not spill. Infrequently, she would hitch a ride by one of my older brothers or one of the country neighbors who went to her church. Most of the time she trudged back home, stopping occasionally to sit on the bank of the road underneath a low-hanging oak tree.

When Effie walked to the store with her kerchief with a knot tied in one of its corners, it was time to treat herself with a surcie. Effie stood at the counter confidently. Like Christmas morning, she slowly loosened the knot, pulled one end through and out, and laid her two shiny nickels on the counter. She slowly turned, walked over to the drink box that purred like a kitten, slid back one of the lids, reached down and grabbed an icy cola, popped off the top with the opener attached to the cooler, and waited before she indulged her thirst. She still had only half her treat. She shuffled her feet over the sandy concrete floor 'til she stood in front of the glass jars that displayed a variety of Tom's cookies, crackers, and salted peanuts. She did not hesitate in making her choice. The infrequent indulgence of her eagerly anticipated treat meant that past experiences had eliminated choice. It was just a matter of doing what she had intended to do for a long time.

Effie carefully removed the top on one of the jars, sat it on the cooler top sitting close by, reached in, and took a tall, thin package of roasted peanuts. She quietly replaced the lid on the jar, walked over to a vacant cane-bottom chair, sat, and rested from her travels. Feeling no rush, she contemplated her anticipated treat. She placed the celluloid top of the peanuts between her front teeth, tore the bag open, placed the bottle between her legs, cupped her hands to make a wide funnel, and poured the peanuts into her tightly held bottle of Coke. There was room in the bottle since she had indulged her thirst with several strong swigs of the secret formula that had a quenching way with thirst like a steady summer rain on dry, tilled soil. All the peanuts in, floating around like a collection of water bugs on the shallow edge of the pond, Effie held her surcie to the light, enjoying the sight before the taste. The long intervals between swigs prolonged the savor. She chewed slowly the peanuts that flowed into her mouth when she drank from the bottle. The last few peanuts that resisted her invitation to exit the bottle would cling to the bottom. Not willing to waste even one, Effie would turn the dry bottle up, beat on its bottom, and force the stuck peanuts out into the palm of her hand. She would chew the last ones even more slowly.

When all were gone, Effie sat for a while. She relished each moment of her treat while grieving the loss, knowing that a repeat performance was much like the fair, coming once each year. The knot in her kerchief no longer needed, Effie lifted it to her face and wiped away any remaining residue. The handkerchief she held gently. A clutch was no longer necessary. Since giving up its treasure, her kerchief became like the others, a piece of cloth cut from a seed or flour sack.

Those who watched might have thought she should have taken some to her mama; she could have eaten more healthily, buying cheese and crackers; she could have paid off some of Ease's store debt. Those who saw and listened with their hearts would have thought, "Leave her alone. She has done a beautiful thing. Momentary indulgence is one of the ways to validate and confirm the value of oneself. Loosen the knot; break the jar. Give yourself a surcie!"

Another Birth

Family

In family it is better to be loved by too many than by too few.

The shepherds said to one another, "Let's go to Bethlehem and see this thing that has happened." So they found Mary and Joseph, and the baby, who was lying in the manger. The shepherds returned glorifying and praising God for all the things they had heard and seen. (Luke 2:15–16, 20)

Effie and I were so different but so much alike. Both our differences and our similarities were like two merging streams that formed a growing friendship. I had older sisters that were more like additional moms than sisters, and so did Effie. The age difference between us and them catered to their growing maternal instincts to have children of their own. It seemed that they wanted dolls more than they did children. They preferred to take us down and out and put us up and away, but we had other needs and plans. We wanted to talk when they wanted quiet; we wanted to be with them when they wanted to be away from us; we wanted them when they wanted someone else.

Effie seemed to have an advantage over me. She had two liabilities that often were her assets. She had a crippled foot and strange fits. Her sisters were more patient, kind, and attentive. I seldom envied that. Effie would have gladly given up what she had to get less, and I did not want what she had to get more. On the farm I always felt that the smallest puppy or leanest baby pig deserved the first and most milk. I could not understand why their siblings didn't see it that way. I was glad to know that Effie's siblings did!

My older sisters, Mary Lou and Kat, like Effie's older sisters, had plenty of children on whom to practice their developing mother instincts. They liked to tell me and all others who would listen the story of my birth. Mary Lou was a young woman of fourteen, and Kat an older child of ten.

It was the time in their lives when Mama's seventh pregnancy was not as unnoticed or as distant as were the others. The previous six had been distinctly hers. Due to their age and interest, this one they shared. Mary Lou and Kat had learned that in due season, birth was as much a part of life as were the changes of the leaves on the sugar maple that stood in the far corner of the yard. Each winter the maple was silently pregnant. In spring she showed the first signs of motherhood as little ones formed on her branches. In summer she grew to be great with child, standing less erect and more stooped and plump. In fall she slowly let them go one by one, like every mother does. With winter, silently her womb was readying for another pregnancy and birth.

Mary Lou and Kat had watched the process of birth. The farm is one great big delivery room. The red maple in the corner of the yard was only one of the mothers who birthed their young in delivery rooms all over the farm. For them it was a time in their own transition from being a child to being able to have a child. They were more interested in giving birth than they were in seeing birth—thus the reason for their three-mile run to see what they had seen and watched before.

It was early fall. The leaves had begun to exchange their dark greens for hints of red and gold. A few had begun to fall gently to the ground, their journey softened by the slight stirrings of the air or even a gentle breeze to separate them from their lingering hold to the branches to float down, down, down till they landed on the grass, building a thickening carpet around the tree. The mornings and evenings were cool, but the day was still unquestionably summer.

It was harvest time on the farm. The peanuts had stretched their arms as wide as they could reach. The roots had anchored themselves to the soil. Out of sight, clusters of peanuts hung to the roots like grapes to a vine. It was time to bring them to the light and hang them around a stack pole to dry in the warmth of the late-summer sun. The soft breezes blew through the stacks, turning the green leaves brown and the peanuts dry.

Harvest on the farm was a family job. Peanuts, like babies, have to be picked when they are ready. Mary Lou and Kat had joined the other older siblings in the field. Ease and Molly, the mule, were slowly moving down each row. Molly pulled the plow that Ease held steady to plow underneath the vines, loosening the soil with the peanuts still attached. It was a dirty, happy job. Dirty because the peanuts had to be shaken and even beaten against the body to loosen the remaining soil. Happy because each vine was a hidden mystery as to how many peanuts it had produced; happy because peanuts meant money for a new dress, a pair of jeans, or shoes for school.

Mary Lou and Kat left for the field early that morning. They had noticed that Mama had not made her biscuits or fried the bacon or even opened her bedroom door. No one talked about her disappearance. Births were frequent on the farm, and everybody knew they were happening, but no one talked about them. There was lots of talk about the product, but there was no talk—just a silent hush—about the process.

Even though no one said a word, there were unspoken words every-where. It's hard to leave the park while the game is being played. But that's the way it is with birth at home. You watch the players warm up and play several innings. Then you leave, only to return to see the final score. Mary Lou and Kat had watched their mama grow. They had watched her play this game several times before. They had been too young to be interested in why there was no bacon or biscuits and why a closed door. This one was different. This time birth was more than an idea, a happening, or even an expected event. This, somehow, was their baby, too, and they wanted to be present for his birth.

It was a long and bouncy trip to the peanut field. The dry weather and the heavy use of the dry, sandy, clay road at harvest time turned the road into a three-mile scrubbing board. Most of the clay dust that was stirred up by Daddy's flatbed truck followed close behind. Sometimes the sun was in full view, but at other times the cluster of tall pine trees kept it hidden. The peanut vines still glistened from the early-morning dew. The leaves of the vines plowed underneath by Ease and Molly the day before were more shriveled and less alert.

Peanut fields come in all sizes and shapes. Some were carved out of the woods years before and were usually small. Others were much younger in age and had been cleared by heavy equipment for planting. This peanut field was expansive and when approached made a completed job seem impossible. Ease and Molly were already working. Mary Lou and Kat had delayed work as long as they could. It was time for them to shake the vines Ease and Molly had loosened with the plow. They worked and thought to themselves, "Is today the day? When will it be? Will it be another boy, or can we get a sister?" These questions, like the vines on every row, were ever present, never far away.

Like Daddy always said, "Work keeps your mind busy." Mary Lou and Kat joined the others, shaking peanuts. They pulled and shook and stacked the peanuts, vine by vine. Each empty stack pole stood tall and thin like mamas do when they are not pregnant. Each pole stacked with peanut vines looked more like Mama now, fat and round. The field was fast taking on the appearance of lots of pregnant moms, all waiting for the right time to deliver.

Kat and Mary Lou were so busy they failed to see Daddy's old truck appear from behind the oaks and pines that hid the winding road from the field. He pulled his truck over to their rows, honked his horn, and said, "A boy." Daddy had a way of keeping his emotions inside and hidden.

He was proud, and they knew it; but he acted as if another birth was like a storm. It, too, would pass, and another one would follow. Besides, this was the seventh storm!

For Daddy it was the seventh but for Mary Lou and Kat a first. They were more ready for Mama to birth this one. It would be more nearly theirs. Daddy drove on, moving to another field where other hands were working in the cotton field. Mary Lou and Kat stood up, looked at each other, and without one word began to run, jumping peanut vines and dodging stack poles. Starting fast, they began their long and tedious journey toward the east, a three-mile journey where they knew a child had been born, and they knew where he lay.

They ran and walked, walked and ran—down the red clay hill, past the creek bottom that breathed its cool air until midday. Mary Lou cried, "Come on! Faster! Let's go!" Kat, the younger of the two but equally as tall as Mary Lou, pushed on. They ran past St. Paul's Church. On they went, past Hector Spann's home place. Stopping momentarily to rest and catch their breaths, they soon moved on past Aunt Donnie's and Uncle Tom's house where Chickey sat on the porch rocking and smoking. Too tired to speak and too anxious to stop, they waved their hands and ran on. Their house was the last landmark. Home was just up the slightly tilted hill.

Mary Lou and Kat had run far enough away from the field to want to stop and rest, but they were close enough to the house to keep going. They were following a star, not in the sky, but in their hopes and dreams. They turned off the recently graded road that ran past the house onto a white, sandy driveway made by Dad's trucks and tractors. Climbing the steep concrete steps that led up to the concrete slab porch, two steps at the time, Mary Lou threw open the unlatched screen door and paused in the long hallway that led past Mama's bedroom. The unpainted wooden door was closed, separating Mama and the baby from the rest of the house and from the world.

Their hearts finally slowed down, catching up with their feet. Mary Lou tapped softly on the door. They waited for what seemed like hours before Aunt Laura, the black, stately, graying midwife, cracked the door. "Just a moment," she said. Then, much like the wind that you feel but never see or hear, Aunt Laura suddenly appeared and opened wide the big brown door. There lay Mama in her bed, cuddling the baby in her arms.

The baby's cheeks were red, his hair thick and wet. He lay there content, at peace, seeming to enjoy his arrival from a nine-month journey. "Bobby is his name," Mama softly whispered while motioning for Aunt Laura. Mama asked Mary Lou and Kat to sit on the bench that sat near her bed, noticing that the peanut dust still clung heavily to their clothes.

Aunt Laura spread a soft blanket in each of their laps. She lifted the baby from Mama's arms, held him to her own breast for a moment, and then laid her prize possession in Mary Lou's arms. Aunt Laura birthed lots of babies, and she acted as if each was her own. For Mary Lou, Aunt Laura handed her far more than a baby. She was holding her future. In holding her baby brother, Mary Lou miraculously changed from being a child and a sister to becoming a woman. For her it was a rite of passage.

"My time," said Kat after stifling her eagerness to hold her newborn brother. She gazed hard and long at me. I was sound asleep. Deep inside of her, but kept carefully silent, Kat thought, "I wish this one were mine." Years passed. Mary Lou married and moved away, and I visited her, spending several weeks at the time. Why not? She had run three miles to hold me in her arms. She was my sister/mama. I was her brother/child. She continued to tell the story of my birth.

Ole Mabel

Presence

Shadows in the dark hold secrets while shadows in the light hold surprises. I have become like a bird alone on a roof. (Psalm 102:7b)

Two are better than one. If one falls down, his friend can help him up. But pity the man who falls and has no one to help him up! Though one may be overpowered, two can defend themselves. A cord of three strands is not quickly broken. (Ecclesiastes 41:9–10, 12)

As a small boy one of my assigned tasks on the farm was to milk Ole Mabel, the cow named after my daddy's sister. Throughout my growing-up years, it was Ole Mabel who supplied us with milk and butter. All the neighbors and the sick of our county drank "Miss Lula's" thick, tasty buttermilk. In exchange for a jar filled with sweet-smelling gardenias, Effie walked home clutching a gallon jug of buttermilk. Clutching because the milk was too prized to spill!

Ole Mabel and I were good friends. When she was good, she and I were best of friends. Occasionally, when she would hit me in the face with her cockle-burred tail or put her foot in the milk pail or kick at me because she was in a bad mood or because I inflicted some unintentional pain on her sensitive udders, we were bitter enemies.

In summertime, sitting underneath Ole Mabel's hot, perspiring body was like standing up against a red-hot, pot-bellied stove. While grazing in the pasture, Ole Mabel would load her long, flowing tail with dry, brown cockle burrs. They grew on waist-high plants, usually on the fringe of the pasture where the tillers left them to grow and produce in early spring. A wad of cockle burrs loaded onto a long-flowing cow tail turns beauty into beast and can become a lethal weapon.

In summer the horse and dog flies followed the cows like small children follow after older brothers and sisters. Wherever the cows go, so follow those mean, circling flies, looking for a place to land, bite, and drink. Smart flies they are, landing on places outside the reach of Ole Mabel's swishing tail. I use my flailing hand or a leafy branch from one of the persimmon trees to fortify her arsenal of warfare against the attacking flies. If the flies chose to land near Ole Mabel's legs or under her fat belly, places that her swinging tail could not reach, she either kicked to frighten them away or took off walking. Her foot would hit the milk bucket and send both the bucket and the milk flying through the air. The milk would drip off both of us.

Sometimes Mabel's foot would land right in the bucket. She would kick again, this time to free her trapped foot, sending me off to the house to get a new, clean milk bucket. When Mom and Dad were not around, I'd take an easier route. I'd rush over to the water faucet hanging off the side of the barn, rinse out my bucket, and try again to finish my tedious job.

In winter a cold, early, frosty morning and a milk cow change a bearable southern climate into a cold, Alaskan winter. There is no place colder than sitting underneath a milk cow. The ground is frozen hard. Our breaths would meet the frigid air, giving off the appearance that both Mabel and I were smoking cigars. Her warm, full bag and the four extended udders were clear evidence that Ole Mabel had worked on through the night to replenish her tank and provide us with the milk we needed for drinking and making cakes and biscuits. The cold of my squeezing hand was a shock to Mabel, but the warmth of her bag and body was a gift to me.

Milking was a tedious afternoon task but one that was not always routine. Mabel's disposition was one factor that kept milking from being routine, but there were others. Some evenings, Mabel would decide to play our game of hide and seek. She would hide, and I would seek. Every morning, Mabel was somewhere near the barn, but evening was different. Most of the time she would eat all she wanted during the day and come home in the evening. If it were a scorching-hot day, she would take a break from grazing and stand in the shade of a pecan tree. Cooled off and rested, she would continue her grazing. When she was eating, Mabel forgot about time. Milking a grazing cow who decides that the clump of grass out of reach is the preferred one is impossible! Forcing Ole Mabel home before she was replete was a task too great for a young boy. And even if I won, her mood would not be the best for milking.

Ole Mabel's quirks and my assigned job to relieve her of her milk were sources of some creative conflict. If she decided to graze late, I still had to milk. If she wanted to stay out late, I had to find her. What she wanted to do and what I had to do were not always compatible. My job required that I be in control even when she acted out her freedom. Even though she produced the milk and I took it, it was my dad who was in control. He was unaware of the level of Mabel's contrariness. He knew the task was done when he found a boiler of milk on the third shelf of the refrigerator. There was no reason for Mabel not to produce milk and no excuse for me not to take it. The only freedom we had was to do our assignments faithfully. There was only one time when I didn't.

There is no reason to explain why a young boy with a dad who expected you to be responsible and knew when you were or weren't would decide to let Ole Mabel have an evening off. She performed twice a day, as faithful as the rising and setting sun. The only time Ole Mabel took days off was when she birthed a calf. My dad always found another cow to take her place, confident that after several weeks she would be back, giving great performances and getting rave reviews. Her butter was so rich and yellow that it created a reputation throughout the county. Reasoning is not why a boy of eight would miss a milking appointment with Ole Mabel.

Multiple factors contributed to my one night of cow-milking delinquency: the growing resistance of a child needing to check out his own emerging powers against his strong father; summer baseball games in the later afternoon where my presence was the difference between having a team or not having a team; the periodic dislike I felt for having to perform daily at a scheduled hour. All created a desire to no-show. The clear consequences for negligent behavior caused me to consider doing my assigned task, but this time I chose differently.

I figured that this particular Saturday night was my best chance because my dad had his nights out with the boys and would be less likely to notice. My dad and Ole Mabel had two things in common: they were faithful and predictable. They both enjoyed a couple nights each year to check out the nightlife. On these nights my dad's spirits were elevated slightly. For me there was the unspoken possibility that if I were going to get by with anything, one of his nights out would be the night.

It could have been any one of the above reasons, or some combination of several, but I failed to show for my appointment with Mabel. Nighttime came, and no one said a word about no milk. I felt some regret, but more fear than guilt. None of my brothers taunted me or took delight in what probably would happen. My mom never suspected that I had taken a chosen vacation. Caring for so many often prevented her from seeing things that did or did not happen.

I took a quick, mostly damp rag bath, jumped into Mama's always clean and well-made bed, pulled the sheet up over my shoulders and head as if to convince myself that this day was done. Tomorrow was a brand-new day. But this day wasn't over yet!

It must have been early morning, but no glow-in-the-dark clock was present to specify the exact time. I just knew it was night, not morning. There above my bed, standing taller than God, was my dad. It was evident that his intention was not a delayed goodnight kiss or even a good morning wakeup. He took my arm and lifted me up and out so quickly that I thought it was the second coming of Jesus that the preacher got so excited telling us about at church. It didn't take much more than the slight opening of my eyes to know it wasn't Jesus and the second coming; it was dad and the first judgment! "Guilty, guilty," I thought, feeling that the darkness of the night, the sleeping state of Ole Mabel, and the age and size of a small boy would certainly call for mercy. Wrong again!

"Son, cows have to be milked twice daily. Get the bucket, and do your job," he said softly but firmly. I'd never milked in my underwear before, and I didn't want to embarrass Ole Mabel or myself. I slipped on my cutoff jeans and headed straight for the kitchen, where I found the milk bucket clean in its place.

The easy part was behind. I could handle my dad and my embarrassment, for both he and it had taken place in the light. There was no darkness greater than the darkness that rolls in and sits still till morning between our house and the barn. There was a light in the barn, but there were miles and miles of darkness between my house and the light chain that switched a sleeping bulb into a glowing light.

My dad, fearing nothing and holding unswervingly to my assigned responsibility, left my room, crossed the hall, returned to his bedroom and bed. As I turned for the kitchen, I glanced out of the corner of my eye and saw him step out of his khaki pants, leaving him in his boxer shorts, his normal dress for bed and sleep. "How could you?" I silently accused my father. Wrong is wrong. I had been taught that repeatedly. My age, my fear of the dark (nurtured in me by my mom, who viewed darkness and evil as good companions), and my steady, good work record ought to give reason enough for one night off. Mercy, not justice, seemed appropriate. Wrong! My dad, much like God according to the preacher, believed in the rules.

My dad, having disturbed my sleep, ready to get his before the early dawn, was of no help. Mama was awake, I knew, but chose not to oppose him and support me, a good choice of her own. My brothers were so sound asleep that not even the second coming would arouse them, much less something I had left undone.

The first part of the journey was not unbearable. I walked toward the barn, looking backward so I could see some light coming from a small lightbulb dangling on an electric cord in the hallway. Its dim light was more like the candle hidden under a basket in the Bible. As I moved more and more away from the light into outer darkness, I felt much like a rabbit in an open field with a hundred circling hawks, each waiting its moment to swoop down and capture its prey. My only protection from the darkness was to walk backwards to the barn. I could see some light shining from the hallway light. Though dim and providing no light for the journey, there was comfort in its presence, for it was the difference between darkness and outer darkness.

God and his presence were not frequent subjects of conversation at our house. I knew God's name and some of the things God did, but they made me cower and fear. I knew—or out of grave necessity, created—God's protective side and repeated to myself, "I am with you. I am with you. Fear not; I am with you." There was some slight consolation in those words, but not much. How could someone I could not see help me when I could not see? My fear made monsters out of branches moving slightly in the night breezes. Bushes that I thought were firmly planted had recently moved to new and different places. Freshly woven spiderwebs felt more like strong fish nets. A distant God and a milk bucket in hand did not make me feel protected from the circling hawks of night. It was just a matter of time! Like the rabbit, I was an easy prey.

Suddenly yet softly, so that my fear did not have time to create or even to react to a creature of the night, my older brother, who felt more comfortable with the night than I, was walking by my side. He said not one word. He didn't have to. He was the light I needed for the dark. He was my distant god, now close by my side, with hands, feet, and face. For a frightened little boy engulfed in the darkness of night, his name was Knocker, which means, "Not alone."

A Limp and Ten Dollars Less

Honesty

Religion and medicine, like the sea and the sand, are close friends, not mates. They keep close company, but the two were never meant to merge into one.

Is there no balm in Gilead? Is there no physician there? Why then is there no healing for the wound of my people? (Jeremiah 8:22)

In Lystra sat a man crippled in his feet who was lame from birth and had never walked. He listened to Paul as he was speaking. Paul looked directly at him, saw that he had faith to be healed and called out, "Stand up on your feet!" At that, the man jumped up and began to walk. When the crowd saw what Paul had done, they shouted, "The gods have come down to us in human form!" (Acts 14:8–11)

My daddy was an enterprising man who was always starting a new business or planting a new crop. He was better at starting a business than he was at managing it. Daddy was first and foremost a farmer. Secondly, he was a pulpwood man, buying, cutting, planting, and hauling to the paper mill load after load of timbers he had cut, tall pines and fat hardwoods. He also opened a country store that was the meeting place for children from all over our small world; children from the north, south, east, and west; children who were white, black, or mixed brown; children of farm owners and tenant farmers; children who were healthy and fast and children who were crippled and slow. Many of their parents traded with my dad at his store. As an owner and manager, there was little difference between cash and credit, a reason why the country store was more a meeting place than a store.

The store sat at the junction of two country roads. One road ran right past our house and ended in a small community called Shorterville. The other ran forever before it merged into Highway 10 near the Georgia line and a small town, Fort Gaines, Georgia. It was a good place for a store. Cars passed by more frequently than any other place in the county. Cars needed gas, and people needed food. Dad sold both.

The store sat far enough back from either road to give us plenty of room to play strikeout, a game we created by using a broom handle and soft drink caps. Three strikes and you were out. The batter scored a run each time he or she connected with one of the pitcher's straight or curveballs with the caps we had emptied from my dad's Coca-Cola box. When someone bought a soft drink and opened it with the bottle opener attached, the caps fell into a container that we emptied often. A thin broomstick and a nasty curveball (cap) gave the advantage to the pitcher.

The playing field we used for strikeout was extended into the roads when we changed the equipment to a solid rubber ball cut in half and either a solid, straight tree limb or an ax handle. With better and bigger equipment, the pitching advantage was compromised. There was no score. The batter was out either by strikeout or if a fielder caught the ball in the air. The batter liked batting because everybody else had to run up the ball. Children are born to hit, not to field!

To the rear of the store was an open field that in times past was ground for peanuts or corn; later, my aunt used it for her garden. It was terraced to keep down the erosion. Store children need space. The kind of space is of minimal importance. The space was perfect for baseball. It was close enough to the store for my older brother to play and to work. He would lock the front door so the customers who knew about our baseball games would come to the back door for service. The game would stop until my brother gave service to the customer and hurried back for his turn at bat or his position in the field. Out of need and friendship our baseball game was racially integrated long before Jackie Robinson.

A baseball field was good business for the store. On hot, humid summer days, after highly competitive games, the players needed both a cool dugout and a refreshing drink. In the store, with Dad's fan blowing cool air and his Coca-Cola box filled with ice-cold drinks, the sweaty players were relieved and satisfied. There was a bathroom attached to the rear of the store, and the door had no sign to designate who could and could not use it. During or after a game everyone needed to go. As I said, my dad was enterprising.

Cokes and crackers were sometimes paid for, but most often each player had a sheet posted on Dad's store wall adjacent to the cash register for credit purposes. The players would make their payments with pennies, nickels, dimes, and occasionally quarters. The credit would be entered and the owed amount decreased. The sheets had far more credits than debits! If most had a coke and a few or one didn't, my dad would make sure all took care of their thirst. In exchange for his kindness, Ellie Mae would sweep the floor or Rusty would refill the Coca-Cola machine. Effie would pick up the paper and cans around the store, and Marilee would restock some of the emptying shelves.

Eddie C. was his real name, but everyone affectionately called him Chester. Chester was a name that clearly labeled his physical condition. All of us watched faithfully the television show *Gunsmoke*. Matt Dillon's sidekick, Chester, walked with a similar limp, dragging his foot much like Eddie C. Eddie C.'s limp was as much a part of who he was as his dark brown eyes and his thick, curly hair. The name was seldom used as a name of derision or as a way of putting him down. It was simply Eddie C.'s identification.

Chester never thought it sensible to mix his limp and baseball. Instead, he chose to build his expertise and reputation around board games, especially pool and checkers. My dad had my cousin Chickey build a checkerboard. It was one of the finest built. We used the soft drink caps for the checkers. They stacked well to make a king. The major difference between checkers and pool was that, in pool, kings could move the full length of the board, either down or across, while checkers could move only one space. When Chester trapped someone with his two kings and moved in to make a kill, he had the same gleam in his eye as Dusty after hitting a homerun or driving in the winning run or driving one over the last terrace and circling the bases at a slow, deliberate pace.

Chester was a northern child. He lived down the dirt road that ran by the side of the store, a road that if you followed it to the end would take you near Georgia. He was the sixth of eight children. His father worked in the woods, not the fields. This meant Chester had lots of free time, and every morning, as steady as the sun, Chester would turn the corner and take up residence at his second home, my daddy's store. Chester was always willing to do chores at the store to earn both his keep and his treats.

There were three children in our community family that had things about them that everyone knew but no one talked about—that is, to children. Ease had talked to me but no one else about Effie's fits, but no one talked about her club foot, how she got it and why she kept it. Mildred was an older cousin who could be visited by adults but not by children and had something called TB. My mama would get Knocker or Hawley to drive her several miles to Aunt Esther's house for her to sit with Mildred. Knocker and Hawley had to sit or sleep in the truck till Mama's visit was over. Mama never talked to us about what Mildred had, believing that was right and best. Not talking didn't help. It made us more curious and scared.

Chester was the third one in our group who had something we saw that made him different. What he had and what had caused it were never discussed. His secret was more silent because he was black and a boy. In the adult world children were to be seen, not heard, and as children we lived by that unspoken rule. (Effie and I were different!) Adults also believed that children were to be protected from the ills of life that were the subjects of whispers, discussions, and talks behind closed doors. The adults, as smart as we thought they were, never seemed to understand that for children, what we did not know was often bigger and more frightening than what we did know.

Chester had something called polio, which left him living but limping. We did know that! For a while we wondered if we could get Chester's disease from playing checkers or eating cheese from the same hoop. Children can stay guarded only for a short time. Familiarity for some breeds contempt. For us familiarity bred buddies, teammates, friendships. Effie had a foot she dragged, and she was a best friend. We were never afraid of her because the foot was a part of her from birth. She was born with two eyes, two hands, one good foot, and one that was club.

Effie and Chester never used their crippled feet as an excuse to lay out or to hang back, to be the runt pig or the weak chick. They were not available to be treated differently or to be the scapegoats for our feelings of weakness or insecurity. They chose not to be weak as a way to make us look better or feel stronger. Instead, they chose to be one of us, and we liked it that way. Their slower pace was worked into the very making of our playful family, like the different farm animals grazing in the same pasture. Eddie C. was a name just like Tommy Lee, Ellie Mae, Bobby Gene, and Effie.

Chester and Effie not only shared a common physical malady; they also possessed a simple, almost silent sense of God's presence. It was either that God's presence favored persons with physical ailments or that persons with physical ailments cultivated the presence of God. Whichever was truth was neither obvious nor important. Chester and Effie both had soft, easy, accepting attitudes about their infirmities. Their infirmities made them better, not bitter. And they handled our questions about God with more ease and sense, as if they lived with the questions we only occasionally asked.

Their common experience created a bond between Effie and Chester. They seldom talked to the rest of us about the origins and conditions of their lameness. They were kind when answering our questions, but they did so with directness and brevity. They were more open and detailed with each other. This came to light one day when I sought to find some explanation for Chester's absence from the store for several days.

Chester's absence from the store was usually due to either illness or one of Chester's occasional visits to an older brother in Florida. The brother sent money for the bus fare, and Chester would disappear for a couple weeks. He would return, not more tanned but more animated for a while about where he had been and what he had seen. His travels gave him a bigger world that he liked to share. It created for us interest and envy. My brother had been to the beach in Florida once, but I hadn't. I tanned from working on the farm. Getting a tan at the beach seemed, if not a better way, a more fun way!

When I inquired, "Does anyone know about Chester? He hasn't been around for several days," the replies were singular, and the same: "No."

Effie handled it well, but her silence made me move in and shoot, not with a shotgun but with a rifle. "Effie," I said, "where is Chester?"

"I don't know," she said. "Maybe he's just not coming around for a while."

Effie and I were friends too, and I knew she had said enough but not all. I would ask for more, but not now.

"Let's play ball." That's all it took. A game was always in the making. It just took breaks. Why put an end to something so much fun? To win and stop was not nearly as important as it was to keep playing. The baseball game simply served as a delay for an answer I had asked about Chester.

Our baseball resumed. If someone wanted to change sides, he announced it, and the negotiations began. The negotiations were as intense as the baseball draft when owners and managers spent hours and days evaluating skills, team chemistry, player risks and liabilities. It was big business. Our team negotiations were as intense as the big leagues, but for a different reason. Players formed friendships that changed as frequently as breaks and timeouts. Friends wanted to be on the same team, and we had to negotiate equal teams based on numbers. If one wanted to change sides, that meant two had to switch. If two, then four, and so on! Social alignment was the cause for most of the change-sides negotiations. They often took as much time and attention as the game. Our baseball games usually lasted until halted by thirst, darkness, or dinner. A longer delay occurred during hoeing, weeding, and harvesting times.

After playing for a while, there was another break, and Effie and I walked off the field together. I returned to my earlier question: "Where is Chester?" Effie told me that Chester had left on Sunday. He caught the greyhound bus to Birmingham, and he was coming home on Sunday.

"Birmingham," I thought. "Where is that? Why would he go there?" I just knew that Chester had gone to Florida to visit his brother. His brother occasionally sent him money to come for a visit. Birmingham! That must be better than Florida!

That was the end of our conversation. My question had been answered, and I was satisfied. I knew there would be more when Chester got home and was back in his normal visits to the store. I forgot about Chester, and things moved on as they do with friends and friendships.

Chester did return. We were more glad about seeing him than we were anxious about his absence. His presence muted the questions about where he had been, why he had gone, and what he had seen and done. Not for Effie! Effie would wait for a more private moment. She had a common interest in Birmingham, and that interest required a follow-up with Chester.

Several days passed. The ballgame continued into endless innings. On this particular day I noticed Chester and Effie hanging back. Everyone else hurried off the field to quench their thirst with either store-bought cokes or store-free water. Others lined up at the bathroom door waiting for a turn.

Effie and Chester saw me as friend, not foe, to their "private common experience." My presence, unlike any of the others, would not change their unscheduled but expected visit. I was neither an interruption nor a participant. I was like the clump of bushes that sat between center and right field, just part of the baseball diamond.

Standing near enough to hear but not to interfere, Effie asked, "Did you go to Birmingham?"

In a low voice and with a drooped head, Chester answered, "Yes."

It was obvious that Chester was more comfortable with unspoken truth and brevity, but Effie moved on. She wanted more, and she knew Chester would tell her more, so she continued. "Was he there?" she asked.

"Yes, but I didn't see him."

"Did he pray for you, and what did you feel?"

It took only a couple questions to prime the pump. There was a well of water flowing inside Chester, and it needed only a couple questions to get the water up and out. It was more like an artesian well, ready to spew forth its trapped waters through any opening.

"My daddy didn't want me to go. He used all kinds of reasons: we don't have the money; where will you stay?; how will you eat?; how will you get to the arena?" Chester had been prepared. His trip was no spur-of-the-moment thing, but clearly the culmination of a thoughtful, well-laid plan. When one has something he wants to get rid of, plans are carefully made, and barriers are only small rocks in a moving stream, unable to stop the flow. The direction of the stream can only be temporarily changed. Chester had saved his money. He could survive anywhere for a few days. Even in a city, auditoriums could be found. The prospect of walking with no limp was far brighter than the darkness of his fears.

Chester had learned about the healing man. Each Sunday morning, he listened to him preach. The man was a good preacher, but what Chester wanted more than his preaching was his healing. At the end of his sermon, he would invite the listeners who wanted to be healed to come near, place their hands on the radio, and believe. He would say, "When I pray, the power of God will come through me, to the radio, on out to you." The man preached on: "The power of God can heal. He raised Lazarus from the dead. He made the blind to see. He cleansed the leper, and he made the lame man walk."

Chester tuned in to listen to the preacher Sunday after Sunday. Not yet confident or even sure about touching the radio for healing, he listened to the preaching and reasoned within himself that God could heal. But doesn't God heal through doctors? With all to gain and nothing to lose, Chester moved closer to the radio with his heart but not with his hand. It took him a while. One Sunday he reached out with both hands, touched the radio, and when the preacher said "Be healed in the name of Jesus," Chester felt something like power go through him. "Could I be healed?" he thought. Too scared to stand and too scared not to stand, Chester stood up, put his weight down on his leg, took a step or two, and felt the disappointment sink into his heart. He was still crippled. But he felt the power!

Encouraged by the feeling of the power, Chester knew he had to go. The healing man was in Birmingham for a healing revival. If the power could come through the radio, just not strong enough for healing, there would be enough power to heal if he could be touched by his hands. Chester started saving his money, counting the days. He was anxious about the trip. He had ridden a bus several times to visit his brother in

Florida, but he was sure that he would be met by his brother. In Birmingham no one would be there. He had to believe. God would be there. Not only would God meet him; God would heal him.

The day finally arrived. The healing services were to begin on Sunday. Saturday was his travel day. His plans were to arrive in Birmingham late Saturday evening, sleep in the bus station, ask for directions to the Civic Auditorium, and catch a bus the next morning, arriving early so he could get a front-row seat. Anxiously, Chester's dad drove him to town, stopping in front of the Central Drug Store on the corner of the square in Abbeville, where buses unloaded and loaded passengers and tickets to everywhere and anywhere could be purchased. His dad once again offered him the option not to go, but Chester's eyes were set on Birmingham.

Chester knew his dad was hesitant and scared to let his son go. They both shared an equal amount of fear and faith. It was difficult not to be a protective parent, yet how can a dad stand in the way of God-preacher healing? For both of them, faith did not erase all doubt. Faith can never be that pure. Faith just keeps on walking when doubt wants you to stop or turn around.

As the bus pulled out of its parking place and moved down the street, Chester's eyes held on to everything familiar until they faded like night in the presence of morning. In their place was the reality of his limp, the presence of his faith, and the diminishing distance between the God of power, the preacher who heals, and his crippled leg.

The bus station in Birmingham was big and buzzing. It was much like the one in Florida, just built differently. Chester found an empty bench spot, sat down (resting his fear more than his body), and ate some cheese and crackers that were inside his brown paper bag, holding all the food he would have and need for his stay in Birmingham. While eating, God made his first appearance to him. It was an incarnation.

An older man from a small town north had ridden a bus to Birmingham for the very same reason. He did not say so, but it was obvious, for he walked with a noticeable limp. Making a trip to get healed is a private matter. Talking about why they were there was not quick to come. It was their common experience, a crippled leg that made public what was private. The older man had already gotten directions to the auditorium and told Chester it was within walking distance.

Night came on quickly but then slowed to a crawl. Bus benches are made for sitting, not sleeping. Too, how could one sleep when a possible miracle was only hours away? Chester felt a lot like Jacob in the Bible. His faith was pinned to the mat as he wrestled with his fears. His faith was climbing a ladder toward heaven.

Morning finally came. The darkness evaporated in the presence of light, much like the dew on the collards by midmorning. Breakfast was both free and closely available. Chester's brown bag, further wrinkled by his unrelenting clutch throughout the night, was slowly unrolled. The bag contained two cold biscuits stuffed with his mama's homemade sausage. They were neatly wrapped in a piece of the white-meat paper my dad used at the store to package the meat bought by his regular customers. It was surprising to Chester how quickly and vividly memories can take one back to warm and familiar places. He didn't linger long with his memories because he and his new friend had to finish eating and get on their way.

Having a walking companion, older and limping, made his fears fade and his faith flourish. The auditorium was only a little bit farther than the store. When they got close enough to see, there was the meeting place, bigger than any barn he had ever seen. Folks were already there, milling around like bees on a honeycomb. Most of the seats near the platform were already taken. They sat down in two folding chairs about midway back in the auditorium. It was good that they got there early.

Quickly, the auditorium filled to capacity and began to overflow. People were standing on the sides and sitting, leaning against the walls. There was a high sense of excitement and expectation as folks came from everywhere, bringing their maladies to be healed. There were also their doubts and faith mixed in varying amounts of unequal proportions. The service began with some announcements and instructions. As the songs were sung, there was a greater stir of anticipation. People watched the side doors, not knowing which door the preacher-healer would use to come onto the platform. When he entered the auditorium, Chester felt his faith leap and his doubts slip away. At the pulpit the preacher-healer was strong, confident, and convincing.

When the sermon was over and before the healing began, an offering was taken. Men dressed in white shirts, dark pants, and different-colored ties lined up in front of the pulpit, and the preacher-healer prayed a prayer that bordered on begging. The men with large collection buckets moved through the crowd, collecting an offering to support the preacher-healer's ministry. When the offering bucket started down his aisle, Chester gladly and confidently reached into his left front pocket and retrieved a folded ten-dollar bill that had been saved and marked for this occasion for months. His ten-dollar bill was soon to reach the bucket for which it had been guarded and saved.

When time came for the healing and all had been made ready, much like a field for planting time, several persons already selected were aided as they came to the platform to be healed. Several others came up from the audience. Chester watched closely as they came with their limps and crutches. The healer man placed both hands on their heads, prayed a fervent healing prayer, and each one walked off unassisted. It was unbelievable. Nothing but a miracle!

It wasn't clear to Chester why some were chosen and others, like him, were not. Each day, he and his older buddy left the bus station and walked to the auditorium, hoping that this would be a miracle day for them. After the first couple services he left still excited and believing. He saw with his own eyes persons like him give up their limps and walk away whole and well.

As the days slipped by and the revival time was nearly over, Chester's doubt returned, and his faith faltered. He had waited so long and had come so far. Would he be chosen? He had seen the healing touch. Even on the last day he held to his hope. At the end of each service, there was a prayer for all to be healed. Chester knew from reading the scriptures that it was the touch that channeled the healing power from God through the human instrument to the sick and lame that made for the healing. If only he could be touched.

At the final service there was a prayer for all to be healed. By this time his disappointment had fed his doubt. His faith that had soared as high as an eagle was now walking with a noticeable limp. Chester came home with his familiar limp, his faltering faith, his expanded doubt, and without his ten-dollar bill.

Takers and a Receiver

Loving Power

If God is all powerful, God is not all loving. If God is all loving, God is not all powerful. God is love. God limits God's power by always using God's power in a loving way.

In my Father's house are many rooms: if it were not so, I would have told you. I go to prepare a place for you. And if I go and prepare a place for you, I will come again, and receive you unto myself; that where I am, there you may be also. (John 14:2–3)

It was one of those cool, rainy days, wet enough to lessen our outside options but not wet enough to close us up inside. One of our options was to dig for doodlebugs. A better option was to climb up into the hayloft and talk. The hayloft was a favorite place of ours, especially on rainy days. It was dry, and the newly baled peanut hay that was stacked almost to the top of the tin roof smelled sweet and fresh. The bales of hay provided us a comfortable place to sit and visit. The wide-open space in the front of the barn loft allowed us to see the farm life without disturbing it. Some of the animals—the pigs, especially—did not mind the rain. They actually delighted in it. My dad said about a pig, "You can clean it up and take it to the fair to win a blue ribbon, but when you bring it back, it wallows in the mud." Cows are different. They delay their grazing and stand underneath the barn to stay dry and warm. Unlike the pigs, they can chew away on their cuds.

It was in the barn loft on rainy days that Effie and I had talked about her mom, Panella, why she was so sad and so alone. We had talked about male cardinals and how more color does not make them "better." It was a rainy day, and I had a question that seemed to be more in my heart than in my head. I had kept it there for a long time, and recently it wanted to get out. When I asked my mom when my baby brother was coming, she replied, "When the time is right." The time was right for my question.

I knew Effie did not like to get her hair wet. The Royal Crown grease she used to hold her hair in place and to make it look kept and shiny did not mix well with rain. Mama kept her pink-flowered umbrella sitting in the corner of the hall next to the front door. I retrieved it and easily covered myself to make the walk down the hill to Effie's house. She was sitting in her sister's bedroom playing with her baby doll. Never in a hurry, she waited for me to get to her back porch, and I waited, as usual, for her to appear. I asked her if she wanted to go to the barn. Since it was her favorite place too, especially on rainy days, she smiled and said, "Give me a minute."

In a minute she returned, and I made a place for her under Mama's pink-flowered umbrella, which Effie called a parasol. Mama's umbrella did not reach out wide enough to keep both of us dry. One side of me got wet, but I made sure Effie stayed dry. The walk was slower, and we had to step together at the same time so we could manage the umbrella. A five-minute walk stretched to ten, but Effie and I had plenty of time, and a slow, dry walk was better than a fast, wet one.

We both climbed the wall ladder that my dad had made to give access to the loft. We found two bales of hay, and we helped each other drag the bales to the opening in the loft. We sat silently for a time, resting from our walk. At first the farm life preoccupied our conversation. After it slowed and ran its course, the time was right for my question.

My mama was a good neighbor, especially at funeral time. When someone would die and Mama was called, she would go and help clean up the body for showing. Often, she would go without a call. She would take her freshly baked, ten-layer chocolate cake. She would add her strong alto voice to the funeral choir. If it was morning, she would make her world-famous biscuits. Sometimes she would just take herself. Mama's presence was a good gift.

My mother's sister, Aunt Vera, one of my favorite aunts, had moved to Florida to a little town that after much work and practice I had learned to spell—Wewahitchka. I would look for an audience to show off my accomplishment. Her son, Thomas, a favorite cousin of ours, spent summers working with us on the farm for board and small pay. A young couple in Aunt Vera's extended family had their first child, a son, who died a few months after he was born. Mama got one of my older brothers to make the three-hour drive to Wewahitchka for the burial.

Mama took me with her to the church revivals and to some funerals. She invited me to go to this one. The ride for me was long but fun because I got to see things other than what one sees on the farm. Funeral rides in our car were always silent and somber. In my family we only talked about "necessary" things. My brother's favorite country music radio station was silenced because, for mama and what she was feeling and thinking, country music and burials were not compatible. All we could do was ride and see.

Boredom for a small boy always gives birth to something creative and fun. I brought out the old travel game of "counting the cows." Since it was not acceptable to play it with the driver and since Mama was not in a playful state, I played the game with "Effie." Effie never *actually* went on long trips with us, like to my married sister's home in Albany, Georgia, but I could bring her with me in my mind. That way I could play the game and keep the silence. I counted cows on my side of the road, and Effie counted cows on the other side. At each graveyard on our respective sides, we had to bury our cows and start over. The one who had the most cows not buried when we arrived was declared the winner. As we approached Wewahitchka, I felt the need to end the game. We were nearing a place where play ceased and sadness began. Effie won 32 to 17!

We timed our arrival so we could go directly to the church cemetery for the burial. There was no church service with preaching and singing like for adults who die. Maybe babies haven't lived long enough to give the preacher much to say and most church songs are for adults anyway. It was a small crowd, mostly family and a few friends.

The cemetery was large and old, and all the buried folks had concrete nametags. Underneath the name, etched in the concrete, were dates of birth and death. Some of the markers had Scripture verses, and others had a line from a song or a poem. The cemetery had a special place for babies. The baby place had a large marker that read, "God's little ones."

There was a hole dug in the ground, and sitting close beside the hole was a tiny brown box that held the baby boy. If he had a name, I did not hear it. The box was covered with fresh flowers. The preacher stood in front of the hole that separated him from the family and friends. When all was ready, I looked at the distant cousin, Tray. Some of the hurting tears that he had kept hidden deep down inside his heart began to trickle down both of his cheeks. I had no tears, but his sad made me sad.

The preacher read some words from his Bible, a big black book. Then he said lots of words. I do not remember any of the words from the book and few of his many words except the words that lingered and formed the question that I was ready to ask Effie. The preacher said that God needed a baby in heaven. He went on to say that on Sunday night God made a visit to the home of Tray and Gayle and took their baby boy to heaven to be with Jesus and all the heavenly angels. It didn't make sense to me that God needed a baby boy in heaven more than Gayle and Tray needed their baby boy on earth. God came and took their baby! I decided sleep was a better way to ride home than to count cows.

The rain continued to fall. The sound of rain on the tin roof provided background music for our conversation. Breaking the silence, I told Effie my story and asked, "Effie, does God really take babies?" As expected,

Effie took her time, and we sat for some time in silence. Effie used the silence, and then she broke it. She had an answer, and she was eager to share it: "In death, life takes. God receives. God does not take babies. God receives them." Effie's answer was so straightforward and firm that I knew two things: she had asked the question for herself, and she had found a good answer from someone else.

Then she told me her story: "After Ma's baby was born dead, I asked Pa if God took the baby. Pa answered my question long and good. It took us more than one sitting. This is what Pa told me: 'God is not a taker. God is a receiver. When God created us, God made our bodies out of dust and used them as a house for the soul. At death the soul lives on, but the house goes back to dust. The house has three takers: accident, disease, and aging. Everything and everybody dies in one of these ways. God created life that way. Do you remember Sam? He was a good hound dog. He and I hunted, and Sam treated many coons and possums. He was a good watchdog. No one could drive up or walk into the yard without Sam barking. One day I noticed that friendly Sam was less than friendly. He was agitated and belligerent. Fearing that he had been bitten by a rabid fox or coon, I locked him up. When he changed into an angry, attacking dog, I knew he had rabies. I had to shoot him to take him out of his misery and to protect you from his disease. Even though I took Sam out of his suffering, if left alone, Sam would have died from rabies. Disease takes lots of animals.

"'You probably don't remember our ol' milk cow Star. Star was her name because she had a perfectly shaped star on her forehead midway between her two curled horns. She birthed calves every year and gave us milk daily. She was nice to milk because she was easygoing and gentle. She was faithful and dependable. Her milk was rich and creamy. Star was healthy and never sick with any of the cow diseases. She got old and older. Finally, her milk dried up, and we had to switch to one of her calves that grew up to be a fine heifer. We kept Star because she was a friend to the family. As she aged, she became less and less mobile and lay in the shade in the summer and stayed in the barn in the winter. One morning I noticed the circling of the buzzards, a sure sign of death on the farm. I walked down into the edge of the woods and found Star stretched out and dead. Star died from aging. If disease does not take, aging will.

"'There is a third taker. Accidents happen on the farm. We had an old goat named Billy. He was a butting goat, so it was best not to turn your back on Billy. He had a strong neck and thick horns. He could butt you down or pick you up off the ground. He was the father of all our goats. Billy was prone to wander. If we left the pen gate open for a second, he watched as if escape were his constant intention. Often, we would have to seek him out after his escape. He would resist capture and fight being penned. He liked to eat the leaves off the blackberry bushes that grew in patches near the road. One day when we couldn't find Billy, I walked up to the road and found him lying in the ditch. He had been hit by one of the pulpwood trucks and killed instantly. Billy was taken out by accident. He was in the wrong place at the wrong time. Some animals die from disease, others from aging, and some from accidents. All animals die. All are taken.'

"Pa went on. 'Effie,' he said, 'people die the same way. Just like the animals die. God does not sit around in heaven checking out who God will take next. Life has its own takers. Before you were born, Grandma Sampson came to live with us. She had lots of children with whom she could live after my dad died. We told her we would add on a bedroom, the one you and Kate now sleep in, and she came to live with us. She was a small woman, very fragile. She had lots of ailments but none serious enough to cause her death. One morning, your ma went in to check on her when she did not get up at her regular time, and your grandma had died in her sleep. She was eighty-two. Your grandma lived a long, good life. She made a peaceful exit. If accident or disease does not take, aging will.'

"'Several years ago Mr. Joe, Bobby's dad, was checking his catfish baskets in the Chattahoochee River. He noticed something floating downstream in the river. First he thought it was a log. As it got closer and closer, he saw that it was a man. He had been floating for some time, because some of his face had been eaten away by the crows. Mr. Joe tied a cord around one of his arms and pulled him to the bank. He tied the cord to one of the tree roots that jutted out into the shallow waters of the river to keep the body from floating on down the river. He finished checking his baskets. He drove to the store and phoned the sheriff's department. The sheriff and the undertaker drove an ambulance to the ol' ash tree where they met Mr. Joe. Mr. Joe led them to the spot where he had tied the body. They rescued the body from the river. Word got out that the man had been fishing in the river near Columbus, Georgia. The boat capsized, and one man in the boat swam to shore, but the other fisherman disappeared. They searched and searched for the body but found none. The body had floated fifty miles in the river before Mr. Joe found him. The man had died in a fishing accident. Accidents take lots of people. Most die in car wrecks, but some die by drowning.'

"Pa got busy and he forgot about the third way folks die, so after some time, since my question was partly but not fully answered, I asked Pa, what was the third way folks die? Pa was ready. He took off and continued on as if no time had passed at all: 'In life, if death does not take one by aging or by accident, death will get you by disease. Most people die from disease. There are so many kinds of diseases, almost a disease for every part of our body. Mr. Jim and Miss Esther had a daughter named Mildred. She got sick. Her family learned after many doctor visits that she had tuberculosis, a deadly disease of the lungs. TB, as it is best known by common folks, is contagious. Mildred had to quit school. She was closed off in a room from her brothers and sisters and friends. She lived until she was nineteen and died. TB slowly took her away.'

"When Pa was finished, he told me that lots of church folks make God the taker. He said that's not so bad if one is old and barely hanging on or if one is suffering and in great pain. God doesn't look so bad. If God takes a young mother or a good teacher or a baby, God doesn't look so good. Making God a taker makes God powerful. Making God a receiver makes God loving. The good book says God is love! Powerful love!"

Country Baseball

Rules

Rules in a game are very much like the banks of a river: they are there to give direction, not to stop the flow.

Since you died with Christ to the basic principles of this world, why as though you still belonged to it, do you submit to its rules? Do not handle! Do not taste! Do not touch! These are all destined to perish with use because they are based on human commands and teachings. Since, then, you have been raised with Christ, set your heart on things above. (Colossians 2:20–21; 3:1)

Do not think that I have come to abolish the Law or the Prophets; I have not come to abolish them but to fulfill them. (Matthew 5:17)

Some children grow up with soldiers and dolls, others with jump ropes and dump trucks, still others with jumping jacks and glass marbles. In my rural neighborhood there were some of all of these, but the game of games was baseball. In the country, baseball is a broad term that includes anything that is hit with a bat, stick, broom, plank, paddle, or handle. The ball can be soft or hard. It can be a corn cob or a cut-off piece of rubber hose. It can be roadside gravel or Coca-Cola caps. The equipment is variable, but the game is the same.

In country baseball there is always a way to score runs, hit home runs, choose captains and teams. The competition can be mild or fierce. Each game can be self-contained, or there can be a playoff and a national championship. The game can be an agreed-upon number of innings, or it can be continued and last forever. When using bottle caps, three strikes and you are out or the sides change from catching to hitting with a flyout. Runs in corncob baseball are scored only by hitting home runs, which means a hit cob has to travel over the wire fence that keeps the animals penned. In gravel ball, outs are only by strikes since line drives or high fly balls can be dangerous or painful if caught. In the country the only things that inhibit the game from being played are number of players and insufficient time. Lack of equipment is never a reason not to start and play a game.

In country baseball, the kind of baseball to be played determines the type of playing field. Gravel baseball is played by a newly paved road or graveled parking lot. Corncob baseball is played near a barn where the hogs eat the corn and leave the cobs for our games. Half-rubber baseball uses a solid rubber ball cut in half. It is a tricky ball that can sail or curve. The field for half-rubber requires enough open space to hit the ball as often and as hard as possible. Since half-rubber balls, unlike gravel and cobs, have to be retrieved, it is best to play on a field that is clear of tall, thick grass and lots of brush and bushes.

Real baseball required at least one Louisville Slugger bat, one beat up cowhide baseball, and was played on a number of fields, depending on who was home team. The store field was the community field and the one most convenient to most of the players. The space was big and open enough but had a terrace that ran from the far corner of left field through center field and down across the right-field line. A clump of bushes huddled together in short right field, offering some restful shade in between innings for some positioned players. Along the outer edges of the first-base line were some plum bushes that in mid-summer provided players with some healthy nourishment. Blackberry bushes made it difficult to retrieve foul balls but also offered their delicious fruit before, during, and after games. Picnic tables and concession stands owe their beginnings to country baseball.

A second field, one more formal and with fewer distractions, was the cow pasture in front of our house. The open space was sufficient enough to accommodate my older brothers, who were hard hitters. Long home runs provided the hitter the baseball privilege to walk slowly around the bases and not worry about running. Our cow pasture was where I learned to chase down long fly balls from brothers who thought singles were not much better than outs and thought home runs were expected. Learning to play deep center field allowed me to catch long balls and come in for short ones. There was plenty of room to roam and catch.

Each baseball field had its own peculiar obstacles. Those obstacles were more a part of the field than the bases. Bases were temporary and portable. Plum bushes and terraces were more established. In the pasture the cow piles that changed from soft to crusty hard were always present. They aided us in developing our "foot-eye coordination" when catching pop flies and fielding grounders. The cows were gracious to move over and let us play, and their field was well-grazed for better play. The cows did leave evidence of ownership of the field by dotting it with brown piles that players stepped over or around. When a player didn't, time had to be called! Cow piles were great encouragers for us to catch all pop-ups and fly balls; otherwise, play had to be called and the only baseball cleaned. Games at this field required far more maintenance. Before play the infield had to be cleaned of all new and old cow piles. The soft piles disrupted the game, and the hard ones caused errors and injuries. The hard ones were often used for the bases since they could be stepped on but not in.

The best field of all was the field that lay close to the high school. It had a smooth, red-clay infield, a grass outfield, and lights that sat on poles high above everything except the school smokestack. I saw the field because one of my older brothers, Lindy, pitched for a class D professional baseball team. This field was their home field. When I went with my brother to the game, I was batboy, retrieving the bats the players laid down at home plate after hitting and running to first base. I was joined by other boys who chased foul balls so that lost balls could be found to keep the game going. Foul balls created a game for the boys. We raced each other to claim ownership of the ball even though we had to give up our find. Adults in the stands would help us by pointing out where the ball had landed.

My first visit to the finer baseball field, I was goggle-eyed at the tall poles that held clusters of lights like a clump of cones on a tall pine tree. During most games there would be a loud explosion, and we would run for cover. Either one of the old bulbs exploded and died and went out with a bang or one of the batters lifted a four ball high enough to cause the explosion. White bases were anchored in the ground. The bases had to be put down and taken up for each game. They were rare collector's items for roaming, searching children in the nearby neighborhoods.

The outfield was closed in by signs that stood side by side, each advertising something most of us wanted and some folks actually needed. Coca-Cola was the biggest and the brightest and was always dead center, located directly behind center field. Next to it was the Wallace Hardware sign with its big hammer and can of paint. There was a simple sign with big red dots, three of them, advertising a liquor store that sold something for older brothers and drinking adults. When I sat on the bench before a game, my eyes would take in all the colorful signs. My eyes would start in left field, move to center, and on around to right field. When my eyes got to the three red dots, I would hurriedly jump it, much like we did the brown piles that dotted and decorated our pasture field. I learned early that red-dot stores were not for children or church folks.

To the right of the Coca-Cola sign were two signs that were more personal to me. One was the sign for the Abbeville Chevrolet dealer, which sold Dad cars, pickup trucks, and pulpwood trucks. Next to it was the Cities Service gasoline station sign. The station's delivery trucks made runs to the country and filled my dad's pumping station with gas for the trucks and tractors and left cardboard boxes of thirty-weight oil. The Chew and Chat sign was one my eyes had difficulty jumping. Those hot dogs, hamburgers, and fries looked real from a distance. Chew and Chat was the only drive-in restaurant in town.

Some of the spaces were vacant, waiting for the local merchants to decide that baseball players and fans buy the products that are advertised on metal fences at baseball parks. They sure impressed me and made me want to buy, especially the Chew and Chat sign! They also helped the balls not get lost and allowed players who occasionally hit home runs to trot around the bases and enjoy the cheers of the fans. The Chevrolet dealership gave a prize to the player who hit a home run over their sign. It wasn't a new car, maybe a discount on an oil change or an air filter.

There was a covered grandstand behind home plate that was wide enough to reach a third of the way down both third and first bases. Smaller bleachers, about ten rows high, picked up there and extended past the corner bases. Two long wooden benches between home plate and third and first bases were where the players and the batboys sat. The home team sat on the bench toward first base and the visitors on the bench nearer third base. It was a field that quickly and often created one of my dreams—not a fantasy, but a dream. One day I would play on this field and not have to worry about clumps of plum bushes and big brown cow piles!

The fourth baseball field was one where we were always the visitors. Just outside the unmarked community of Shorterville was the school for the blacks. As a young boy I never understood why it was all right to play ball there but not all right to go to school there. Since it was the blacks' school, it certainly made sense that we were always the visitors. The invitation to play the game was only once each summer. It was a big game between the white boys up the road and the black boys from Shorterville and surrounding areas. Not all the white boys played baseball, so it was a hard task to find enough to field a team.

Even as a first-grader, I remember being stuck out in right field. If I could not catch the ball, I could chase it down. It was a good thing I knew something about baseball, but I didn't know everything. As a seven-year-old it never occurred to me that I was inept or underdeveloped. I thought my older brother was protecting me when he moved me from right field to left field each time one of their batters hit from the left side. I was never consulted about the move. I felt so proud to be on the field that I didn't give much thought to where I was located. He could have put me in his shadow at first base and I would have thought my position was as crucial to the game as his. Playing was what I liked. Where I played didn't matter till much later!

This playing field was rated "B." The high school field was "A." The store field was "D," and the pasture "C." The "B" field had a tall chicken screen backstop, which sped up the game from a slow crawl to a slow walk. It had no obvious obstacles like plum bushes and persimmon trees, but it was less than smooth like the high school field. It was more like a rough, dry cob. The outfield was spacious and open, and its grass was high and thick since there were no cows to graze. Singles stopped just beyond the bases; fly balls had room and reason to travel long and far. One great big shade tree stood to the third-base side of home plate, giving the home team a shady, cool place to stand or sit. The visiting team kept sweating in the hot summer sun, giving us what I would call a disadvantage. The one shade tree was big enough for both teams, but I learned later that it was the intense competition, not the color, that kept the teams apart.

Country baseball is an everyday game. The playing fields were left vacant when work called or when there were too few players. The black school field was a weekend or holiday field. The players were older, and their games were played on Saturday afternoon when even farmers and pulpwooders took a break. Or the field was used on July 4, the only summer holiday.

What made playing the game on July 4 different was the game brought in some fans. It was a part of the Independence Day celebration. Barbecued chicken and goat were served with two slices of white lite bread, a cup of Brunswick stew, an iced down Coca-Cola, and one of the store's great big "penny" crackers. The charge for the meal was $1.25, but hunger and plenty of notice kept even the poorer folks from being without enough change. Fourth of July brought forth from every pocket five quarters for a plate of barbecue. It was enough to satisfy one's hunger and get the crowd ready for the game. Children ate free, and most didn't want the cup of Brunswick stew!

For a first-grader it was a Yankee Stadium setting. My only worry was that there would be enough big boys or older children for my brother to move me from right field to batboy. I would be disappointed but still proud to be one of the white boys from up the road. Whether I was playing right field or picking up bats and chasing foul balls, I was preparing for making my dream come true.

Along with the field and two teams, even country baseball had to have an umpire. We had two who were experienced. They were umps not because they were good but because they were willing and available. Both teams needed umpires more than umpires needed teams!

Hector never saw a weekend or holiday except through bloodshot eyes. He had reached a level of drinking that made no distinction between store-bought or home-brewed liquor. Hector needed whiskey, and where he got it depended more on cost than on quality. Whiskey was part of the reason Hector liked umpiring. It freed him from having to call it right and gave him a sense of control and authority. When Hector umped, Hector was in charge!

Hector devised his own way of keeping things right. He marked balls and strikes in the dirt, a small spot he cleaned after each batter, and he marked with a stick he found underneath one of the pine trees. His protection was his whiskey and the extra face mask that belonged to the team up to bat. An intoxicated umpire seldom made a bad call. What he said was what it was. Arguments were little more than expressed feelings and delay-of-game tactics. He was always right even when he was wrong and the players and coaches wrong even when they were right. Hector liked his whiskey; his umpiring role, which afforded him status and power; and the audience, which readily changed from jeers to cheers on almost every called pitch or play.

Peter was the second of the available two-man umpiring crew. He was much younger than Hector and much bigger. Hector was thin, tall, and skinny and referred to by those who disagreed with his calls as "bony blind." Peter was not just big; he was massive. If Hector were a pickup with an extended body, Peter was a pulpwood truck, fully loaded. His hands looked like Mama's fan-shaped running rose trellis that stood at the edge of her flower bed. His body looked like one of the water oaks that shaded our front yard long before we lived there. His feet left footprints on the field that would have raised suspicion of some wooded monster if we had not been there to see them made.

Peter's body was unquestionably man, but his mind had not developed to keep pace with his body. He was an older child housed inside a grown man's body. His size gave him the authority to be in charge and his mind the freedom to be unpredictable. Country baseball had rules, but they could be set aside or gone around or even ignored, and Peter had a reputation for doing all of the above. It made for more arguments, but at least the game always carried an element of suspense or a moment of surprise.

Hector liked wearing the extra face mask and crouching down behind the catcher. He felt more confident when he had the game out front and he could see it all. He could be in charge of everything! Peter on the other hand tended to flinch and turn his head on every pitch, so he chose to stand on the edge of the pitching mound behind the pitcher. That way he did not have to wear a mask, and he thought his eyes could see better and more clearly. The scared child inside his grown man's body did not like the foul tips that occasionally missed the catcher and found the umpire. The slightly elevated pitcher's mound slightly elevated him and his sense of power and authority.

Barbecue dinner under the belt, fans sitting in chairs and on crates under shade trees, both teams warmed and ready to play, and the last-minute appearance of the umpire (Peter liked to make a grand appearance), the game was on. Peter had arrived early for the festivities, for one of the benefits of umpiring the game was all-he-could-eat barbecue. That turned out to be good pay for a few hours of work, especially for Peter!

The white pitcher for the big game between the Shorterville Stars and the Wesley white boys from up the road was a big, overgrown boy we called Hank. Hank had an older brother, Al, who was a pitcher, and he worked hard to make Hank one too. Even though Hank was more inclined to mechanics, big brother Al worked hard to sharpen his pitching skills. Frequently as we rode past their house on our way to and from the corn and peanut fields, Al would be working hard to get Hank ready for the next game. Hank practiced pitching from a homemade mound that was nothing more than several buckets of red clay that Al had dug from the washed-out gulley near their house. The clay had been rounded and packed to give some elevation. Al wanted to give Hank some game-like practice.

Hank was big and strong but lazy. Brother Al knew that Hank could be a good pitcher if he practiced often and hard. Hank wanted to be a good pitcher but not if it meant "often and hard." Consequently, Hank's pitching was fast but out of control, as unpredictable as Peter's umpiring.

One of my older brothers, "Blackie" (because of his dark coloring and hair), played first base. Unk, my mama's half-brother, who was younger than most of her children, was the catcher. He covered his chest with a thick breast protector and his shins with hard plastic that buckled around his legs at the top near his knees and at the bottom near his ankles. He squatted behind a piece of plywood that had been cut into a small square for home plate.

Al was on third, positioned about six feet east of a burlap bag filled with some sand from our front yard. Playing third kept him close to Hank so he could visit the mound often to give Hank advice regarding different hitters. Knocker was in left field; I was in right. The major difference between the two of us, other than our positions, was Knocker was in the lineup because of a shortage of players. I was there because I wanted to be in right field, the position reserved for the worst player, but I was convinced that it was because of my age. Rusty, a light-skinned black boy, played second. The other team's area of recruitment was more populous than ours, so their team was all black.

Out of necessity our team was slightly integrated. Thomas, a cousin from Florida who worked with us on the farm during summer, played short. The center fielder was Tommy Lee, unquestionably black, who was the last to be added to the lineup. The batting order was printed on the back of a brown paper bag and nailed to a nearby tree so we could keep up with the batting lineup. Tommy Lee's promise to be present for the game was as unpredictable as Hank's pitching. I kept looking down the road to see if another late player might show and I would be demoted to batboy. "Whew," I sighed as Hank finished his warmup tosses and big, bad Peter cried, "Batter up!"

I pulled my Farmall tractor cap down to shade my eyes, bent over at the waist with my hand and glove on my knees, looking more like a baseball player than I actually was. I needed to impress the biggest baseball crowd in my life as well as assure my older brother that he had done right by putting me in the lineup. If I looked like a baseball player, maybe they would not try to hit balls to right field.

The first batter for the Shorterville Stars was Pee-Wee McCallister, named that because he was shorter than most men. He batted first because it was hard to throw him strikes. Hank, trying to work out some of the first-inning jitters, walked behind the pitcher's mound, breathed a few deep breaths, spit on his glove several times and massaged it in, spit on his pitching hand and massaged it in, and toed the rubber mat that had been cut from one Mama had used at her front door before she bought a new one with pretty dogwood blossoms. Nervous before the first pitch, Hank stepped off the rubber and scooped up some dry, red clay and used it to powder both hands. By now Hank's delay had challenged Peter's authority, and he said in a loud voice for all to hear, "Okay, boy, let it fly."

Hank's first pitch was no surprise. It was several feet inside, and Pee Wee had to do a fast, high-stepping dance to keep from being hit and seriously bruised. Pee-Wee's anxiety after the first pitch was greater than Hank's. He backed out of the batter's box. The hard, inside pitch left Pee-Wee so shaken that he went over to the shade tree and picked up another bat and tried it out with a few swings. Finally, Pee-Wee had challenged Peter's control of the game as well as his patience. "Come on, Pee-Wee. It'll be dark before we get to the second batter!" Pee-Wee stepped back in, tapped the loose plywood plate with his different bat, adjusted his pulpwood hat, and got ready for the second pitch. It was high and way outside, bouncing off the tightly strung chicken wire.

"Ball two!" boomed Peter. The next pitch was quicker. Hank was still anxious, Pee-Wee less scared. The pitch was low and outside. "Ball three," said Peter, holding up three big fingers on his fan-shaped hand. Hank walked Pee-Wee on four pitches. His first strike came on the third batter. The number-three hitter in the lineup fouled off a pitch, delaying the game while a fan retrieved the ball near the barbecue stand. Hank's anxiety lessened, and his pitches were closer, but he walked the third batter on a full count to load the bases. By this time I had decided that right field was no less exciting than third base because the only two players with any action were Hank's pitching and Unk's catching. Unk was catching a few but retrieving most of Hank's pitches that caromed off the creosote post or bounced off the tight chicken wire. Al walked over from third and gave Hank more pitching advice than he wanted. Peter, again challenged, walked out toward the mound and said, "Come on, man. We have nine innings to play!"

There was no way to know or to predict what was soon to happen because none of us had ever seen or heard of it—not even in country baseball! The bases were loaded, no one out. Hank's control had gotten better with each batter. Pee-Wee saw no strikes, not even a close one. Hoot Grimsley saw a couple close ones, but Peter saw them as balls. Hank had run the count full on John Williams but lost him to load the bases.

The fourth batter and cleanup hitter was big and strong and struck out about as much as he connected. Tucker stood over six feet tall. He had a neck like an ox, and his arms looked like the lower limbs growing off one of the oak trees in our yard. Hank had only one pitch, and that was a fast ball. He toed the rubber, checked the three runners on base, rocked, and fired a fast ball that Tucker couldn't resist. It was high and slightly wide, and Tucker's bat cut through the air like a bolt of lightning. The crowd let out a harmonious "ah," and a whisper broke through the crowd like a dark secret told at a pea-shelling. It was the game's first exciting moment.

The crowd turned from their other interests and focused solely on the batter and the pitcher. They waited impatiently to see who would own the white baseball that had now picked up a few scars from bouncing off the creosote post and the chicken wire. Hank stood on the mound looking for Unk to flash the signs. All of us and all of them knew that Hank had only one pitch. Tucker waved the bat back and forth. He crouched over at the waist, cocked the bat over his head, and waited. Hank kicked and fired. "Ball," hollered Peter, making sure the captive crowd was aware that he was in charge of the show. The tension was mounting.

Lots of runs in the first inning would turn the game in their favor and put us in the familiar role of catchup. Hank stepped off the mound. Tucker stepped out of the batter's box. Knocker turned and watched some martins chase a hawk across the bright blue sky. Al continued to loudly coach Hank on how to pitch. Tucker stepped back in. Hank toed the rubber. The crowd fixed their eyes on the closing distance between the start and stopping point of each pitch. Unk flashed his signs. Hank fired his fast ball, and Tucker watched it sail high and wide. "Ball two!" cried Peter, holding up two long, fat fingers high above his head. The crowd relaxed and settled back like a yo-yo on a string, resting at the end, pausing for a split second before climbing once again.

Hank stayed on the mound, Tucker in the batter's box. The tension had risen to the point that neither felt further delay was in his favor. Hank twisted the ball in his glove, searching for the seam. Tucker waved the bat. Unk rocked back on his heels. Hank surprised everyone except his pitching coach. Hank slowed the pitch. Tucker stood frozen! All his weight, size, and power stood still and watched the changeup float like a leaf, aided by no stirring breeze. Still, just like the leaf, there was no control. Hank's surprise pitch floated off to the side. "Ball three," said the umpire softly, as if to tone his voice to fit the pitch.

Hank, pleased that his pitch had caught Tucker by surprise but disappointed that it had drifted outside, walked off the mound. Tucker quickly stepped away from the plate as if to hide some of his embarrassment for being fooled by the pitch, making him like a helpless deer frozen in headlights. Brother Al stood still with a frozen smile on his face, knowing that he was the source of Hank's new pitch. The crowd was more relaxed, expecting another walk and a boring way for any team to score a run.

Hank quickly positioned himself for the next pitch. Tucker stepped back, determined not to be surprised again, or walked. Hank fired his fast ball. Tucker swung and met the air with such force that his twisted body, like a pretzel, ended up kneeling on the ground. "Strike two!" said Peter, slowing his call down to build the drama and draw attention to the director of the show. Ball three. Strike two. Tucker dug in. Hank dug in. Hank stared down Tucker. Tucker stared back. Hank swung his arms above his head, pushed off the mound with his left leg, and let go of a fast ball that sailed far off to the right. The pitch was so far outside it offered little temptation for Tucker to swing or give the ump any reason to make a bad call. "Ball four," said Peter, indicating his disappointment over the prospect of a long and tedious afternoon.

Tucker dropped his bat and took a step toward first. Pee-Wee was about halfway home with the first run of the game when Peter raised his hands above his head and stopped the game. For a moment all of baseball stood still in its tracks. Peter walked out from behind the plate and firmly motioned Pee-Wee to go back to third. He called to Tucker to stop, and then as if baseball had always been played that way, said to Tucker,

"Go over there and sit on the pine tree stump. When we get a base open, I'll put you on."

A stunned silence was followed by a brief, intense protest that disappeared almost as fast as it began. Al had protested the most profusely, feeling some need to be more openly supportive of Hank's pitching. Peter called the game, enforced the rules, and occasionally created new ones. The game continued. Hank pitched. Brother Al instructed. Tucker rested on a pine tree stump. Knocker watched the martins chase a hawk across the sky. I stood in right field dreaming my dream, and Peter called the game and ran his show. And country baseball went on.

Queen

A Name

Be careful what you name a child. It might be too much or too little.

A good name is more desirable than great riches; to be esteemed is better than silver and gold. (Proverbs 22:1)

Lift your eyes and look to the heavens: who created all these? He who brings out the starry host one by one and calls them each by name. (Isaiah 40:26)

She will give birth to a son, and you are to give him the name Jesus. (Matthew 1:21)

My cousin Chickey, who was always grown to me and never a child, lived a quarter of a mile down the red-clay road that ran a short distance in front of our house. Chickey was single and unemployed because of his need for freedom and independence and his peculiarities. He worked periodically at odd jobs that began and ended on his time and his terms. He was the most self-employed person I ever knew. He must have earned good wages because he had a billfold as overweight as he. If I had not learned early that only women have babies, I would have thought that Chickey was giving birth continually. My older brothers envied his independence. "Look," they would growl as they headed back to work in the fields. There Chickey sat, his feet propped against the pillars of the porch, rocking back and forth in one of the brown, unpainted rockers that lined Aunt Donnie's porch.

One of the reasons Chickey's billfold was so fat was because he did many different things that brought him money. He was a builder and a carpenter. He raised hens that laid big, brown eggs that he sold to neighbors and friends and at the store. He raised watermelons and cantaloupes. He had neat, white beehives from which he collected pure, golden honey, which he sold as fast as he could get it. It was from cousin Chickey that I learned about bees.

Each beehive had hundreds and hundreds of worker bees. They flew all over the countryside, enslaved in their search to find sweet syrup from all kinds of flowers and shrubs to make honey. Each hive had only one mother, and she was called the queen bee. The worker bees did all the work while the soldier bees maintained a constant watch. The worker bees gave their lives to build the queen's castle with many rooms and filled each one with sweet, golden honey. The soldier bees gave their lives to protect her. She was born to be a queen, and a queen she was!

Queen, Effie's sister and my friend, like the queen bee, was born to be a queen. Her name was an affirmation of her birth. Her life situation was a denial of her name. Her name was an expression of hope born but not found. The prettiest of Effie's sisters, Queen was different. She moved about with an air of importance. She was regal and stately. She also carried inside anger for having to settle for too little when she was born for so much—to be named a queen and to work as a maid.

Queen was neither black nor dark brown. Nor was she white. She was golden. She looked queenly when she swept the floor or milked the cow, when she picked peas or shucked corn, when she fried chicken or made chicken and dumplings, when she made a bed or ironed a shirt. Her beauty matched her name. She was the oldest, and more was expected of her. She moved about and traveled in larger circles, yet she could never be the name she carried so well.

To Effie and me, Queen was her name. It was what made her different from Kate or Pearl or Belle. To us her name was a designation, not a description. Her name was a title, not an expectation. Like Effie and Bobby, she was Queen.

Queen was a masterful artist. It was amazing what she could do with Effie's hair. Sometimes when I would drop by to visit Effie, looking for something to do or someplace to be, Effie would be sitting at Queen's feet, leaning back against her lean, lanky legs. Queen would be busy making one of her art pieces. Using Effie's hair, some Royal Crown hair grease, and various sizes of brown paper torn from one of Dad's grocery bags, I stood still, amazed at what she was doing or at what she had done.

Unlike my hair, which had only a couple minor variations caused by the sleeping position of my head, Effie's hair was like the weather, changing all the time. Effie would sit, almost motionless, for what seemed to be hours. I wanted to play and go, to do something. She wanted to be played with, and Queen gave her what she wanted. Effie was patient, and Queen was a perfectionist. Sometimes I left. Other times I was so fascinated by what was forming and shaping that I sat or stood and watched.

Queen was also a generalist. Like the family doctor who treated everybody and everything, Queen liked variety. Effie's hair was her canvas, and the picture that took shape was as much a surprise to the artist as it was to the audience. Sometimes Effie's hair looked like a field of corn stalks without any ears or foliage. Each wad stood tall and erect. It was held that way by the thick, greasy Royal Crown hair dressing that Queen applied with her fingers and combed in with her black snaggletooth comb. Sometimes Queen collected bunches of hair. By winding the hair back and forth between her fingers, she plaited tiny pigtails that sat on Effie's head like a new litter of pigs viewed from behind.

Occasionally, Effie's head grew big like one of Daddy's prize watermelons. Queen would fray each hair by drawing it back and forth through the comb. Her head grew from normal to oversize. Her head looked like the end of a rope where each strand had separated from the other, curling up and out to look like a fluffy ball. Infrequently, Queen would impose her creation over Effie's resistance and make large plaits that lay close to her head, making her hair look like a freshly planted field where the rows hung close to the ground, lying close by each other, silently undisturbed. Each row was perfectly spaced, and where there were no rows, there was Effie's clean, exposed scalp.

Queen was not only an artist; she was a craftswoman. One of her specialties was making pop-gun poppers. She earned the reputation of being the best popper-maker in our end of the county. Effie and I wanted one, and we wanted the best. Younger brothers and sisters had to wait to own their first popper. We waited our turn. Queen could not be rushed, and she worked her own hours. We were ready to belong to the proud army of pop-gun owners. To own one was to belong.

The chinaberry tree grew next to the south end of Effie's house. It was a big tree. We used it for climbing, and the birds used it for nesting, and they often sat on its branches to practice their music. The yard underneath it was clean, gray sand. It was often swept using one of Panella's sage brush brooms. Effie and I often sat in its shade, making sandcastles and dream houses with our hands and feet. In late summer the tree would share its chinaberries with the birds and squirrels and with our brothers and sisters who used the berries for ammunition in their pop guns.

The tall, thin cane reeds grew near the creek. They grew in clusters, not like other trees that settled everywhere. The cane reed family, like ours, was of different heights, shapes, and sizes. Most of them were adolescent size. Some grew tall and round, and others were young and thin. The midsize canes were favorites not because they were better or stronger, but because they were a more suited size for making barrels for our poppers. Choosing one was not easy. It was like choosing a marble out of a jar. All are much the same size, but each one seems to be better than the rest.

Effie and I were allowed to choose our own. Queen carried the ax on her shoulder. We ran from cluster to cluster, picked this cane and that one, delaying a hasty decision, for we wanted our popper to be the best.

Settling on one I exclaimed, "This one is mine," pointing to one of the midsized ones. I was young enough to believe that a larger one was always a better one. Effie, older and wiser, kept looking. Finally, she encircled a smaller midsized one with her hand and indicated to Queen that it was the one. Queen cleared away the underbrush for cutting purposes and with one or two quick, accurate swings laid my reed softly on the ground. Effie's fell with one sharp blow.

Queen stepped back, raising the ax to her shoulder. Walking toward the road that ran beside Effie's house, she let us claim full ownership of our selected reed by letting us pull and tug them through the thick under-brush out into the open space. She gently but quickly trimmed away the branches, leaving only a tall, thin reed that we easily carried with both our hands. Each reed personally chosen, Queen would soon transform them into our personal guns. On each side of the reed gun, Effie and I would carve our initials. Our initials guaranteed that our guns would not be stolen; if they were lost, they would be returned to their rightful owners. Pop guns were toys seldom shared!

Queen sat in a straight-back, cane-bottomed chair underneath the chinaberry tree. We sat close by, watching her every move. She cut, trimmed, and scraped until the reed barrel was as smooth as silk. As the outer skin was scraped away, our reeds slowly turned from a dark to a pale green. Queen told us its skin would get harder as it dried and would turn to a golden brown. Each of our barrels was about two of Effie's feet in length.

Queen finished shaping the barrels and with a piece of stiff clothesline wire she pushed out the soft marrow from inside the cane reed barrel. The inside stuff looked like and felt like one of Mama's broken-up sponges that she used to clean the kitchen and bathroom sinks. Holding up each barrel to one eye, she kept pushing the wire back and forth. Finally, when she could clearly see the water bucket without any interference, she knew the barrel was clear and that part of her craftsmanship was finished.

Laying each barrel on her empty chair, Queen got up and motioned for us to follow. We went over to the persimmon trees that also grew in clusters, growing near the washed-out gully just above Effie's house. It was one of our fun places to play. We made water fountains out of its banks when the ground was soaked with either heavy rain or several days' rains. We slid down the taller banks on pieces of cardboard boxes. We threw persimmons from one side to the other and kept score as to who caught the most. Soon we would see who could shoot chinaberries across its wide-open arms. We had watched others shoot across, and soon we would shoot our own initialed guns.

Just as a wagon is not much good without a mule, a gun barrel is of little use without a popper. Queen had used the persimmon branches before and knew that they were both durable and pliable. The branches were easily bent but not easily broken. The persimmon poppers were plentiful and perfect. They, too, came in all sizes. One was bound to fit!

Effie and I stood close to Queen as she chose branches that she thought would fit and followed her as she took more than needed and laid them on a cut-off plank that lay under the edge of the house. Using her ax, Queen trimmed the persimmon branches and cut them a little bit shorter than the two-foot barrels. Queen's chops were shorter and her aim true. She handed to Effie and me several of the right-sized branches. She propped her ax against the house and returned to her chair and sat. She motioned for each of us to bring her both our barrels and our branches. She reached for mine first. Effie seemed to understand that working on my gun was not favoritism. It was simply a courtesy, acknowledging me as a guest.

Queen rose from her chair and went into the house to the kitchen to get a knife for forming and shaping our poppers. The handle of the knife was as long as the blade. The handle made the knife look old and used. Ease kept the blade looking new and sharp with his metal file. He would sharpen and sharpen, stopping occasionally to run his finger softly across the blade to check out his progress. If it had not reached his satisfaction, he would continue to stroke back and forth, back and forth. When his touch met satisfaction, Ease would lay the knife aside and reach for another. Sharpening knives was something Ease did well and often. Ease didn't like to talk; he liked to work.

Queen used the sharp butcher knife to trim away the smaller branches and to scrape away the tender outer bark on the persimmon branch she was fashioning to fit the hollow reed. She was careful not to make the branch too small, because the tighter the fit, the better the gun. When the fit was too tight, Queen would reach for some of Ease's axle grease that he kept handy to use on his wagon wheels. Placing the grease in the palm of her hand, closing her hand, she would pull the branch back and forth, greasing it from end to end. The branch cleaned and greased, she would move it back and forth in the cane barrel until its resistance almost disappeared. Getting the fit perfect, Queen laid the popper aside to dry and harden.

"Can we shoot it now?" I asked. "Not yet," she answered softly. "A gun is not yours until you initial it. Then it is yours forever." Making something yours is like being born. What makes you different is the name you were given. A baby is just a baby till it has a name. Then it is one-of-a-kind. So it is with pop guns. Queen had made many pop guns. She could see them finished from the time she started. Effie and I were so eager to be owners that we wanted our guns finished soon after we started.

Effie, older and more experienced in making her letters, worked on her barrel alone. She carved her initials clearly and neatly. Queen took a pocket knife and etched a dim "B. M." on my barrel. She showed me how to push the point of the knife over my initials. Soon "B. M." sat on my barrel, clear as could be. It was as if I had been born again. My initials on the barrel made it mine, much like my name made me, me! When the barrels were finished, Effie and I sat gazing at our treasures, holding them in our hands like you do a baby bird, firm but not too tight.

Queen pointed to the gray tin roof that sat on top of the smokehouse. "Let's put them up there during the daytime so the sun can dry them out. Effie can take them down at night and keep them in her room." With my initials on the barrel and my gun in Effie's care, I was satisfied. I knew we could check them out each day. And we did! We watched as the poppers changed color and hardened. Finally, Queen gave us the green light, telling us that the poppers were ready and the guns belonged to us. Her last advice was not to shoot them at anyone.

The barrels had poppers. The poppers had barrels. But a gun is not a gun without ammunition! The chinaberry tree was loaded with berries. Too green for the birds and the squirrels, they were just right for two new, initialed pop guns. Effie and I rushed to the chinaberry tree. Its branches grew near the ground. I was tall enough to reach a few of the berries. Effie was tall enough to fill her pockets and kind enough to help me fill mine. Ka-pop, Ka-pop, Ka-pop, Ka-pop. It was like the Fourth of July without color.

Effie was good at making up games. "Let's get a bucket from the barn and see if we can ring it," she said. With practice more and more berries collected in the bucket. Too easy, we agreed, and thought of other games to play with our guns. A smaller can. We chose one of the smaller oak trees as a target. We drew a circle in the sand and got a point for each berry that landed and stayed inside. Soon our games changed from targets to distance.

I turned to aim and shoot. "No, no," cried Effie. "Don't hit the hens. It hurts and scares." I felt so ashamed. Shooting one of Effie's hens was like shooting her. With Effie when I did wrong, my shame was painfully present, but it seldom lingered. It was like the spring showers—quick and heavy at times but soon gone and forgotten.

Effie had a way of moving on. She did not stay with things that tended to hurt and to separate. Being together—chasing butterflies, making dreams from fluffy clouds, catching June bugs—was more fun than being hurt and apart. Effie's presence was like the sun; it warmed and melted things away. She was like the wind, which blew gently and moved things out and on. So it was with my shame; it lingered for a moment, dissolved, and disappeared.

Our guns were our constant companions. We played with them daily and protected them at night. That was the way it was with our friendship. A new toy, a new game, a new task got our full attention for a while and then faded. Our guns kept popping, but we were too interested in many things to get captured by any one thing. We played the old games with our pop guns, ringing the water bucket, shooting the greatest distance, hitting the changing targets.

Then we created a new game. It was much like the game of holey marbles that I played with my brothers. Instead of holes, we made circles. Sweeping away all the leaves and sticks and excess chinaberries with Panella's sage broom, we drew five circles in the swept sand, three in front of the starting line about ten feet apart and two off to the left side, ten feet apart, forming an L shape. The person who shot chinaberries into the five circles, going and returning, was declared the winner. Instead of holey marbles, we called our new game holey berries.

As summer slowly slipped away, so did our supply of chinaberries. As the supply dwindled, so did our use of our guns. We shot more infrequently and chose our targets more carefully. There was fierce competition for the scarce berries of early fall. The birds ate the softer ones, and the squirrels began to store food away for winter.

Each of us carried our guns like babies softly sleeping. The season was fast closing, and like the star of Christmas, our guns would soon be put away until another summer. Sometimes a little boy wants to be mischievous. Effie had scolded me when I had aimed a shot at one of her friendly hens, and I had felt shame and sorrow. On the last day of shooting, it seemed that every one of her hens walked by, daring me to shoot. I wondered to myself, "How good a shot am I? I've never hit a moving target."

I stood wanting to do what I shouldn't and wanting to do what I could. Effie had a way of always being present even when absent. I knew she would soon return, and that awareness kept my behavior lined up with my "better" person. Temptation has a way of undressing and redressing in a hurry. I saw Effie walk out of the house and on to the small porch that was a walkway from the house to the kitchen. I knew she would be coming my way.

The temptation was stronger than I ever imagined. Effie would be surprised. I had never shot a moving target. The gun that I had held daily for the full summer would soon be gone for a season. I had three berries in my pocket. The temptation was too much for a little boy. I had to do something I had never done before—surprise Effie!

I saw her foot drag down the steps. Looking under the house, I could see her start the short journey around the kitchen to the side of the house where chinaberries grow for birds, squirrels, and little boys with pop guns. Carried by the excitement of my plans, I moved quickly, without any thoughts of wrongdoing. I was no longer in charge of my plans; my plans were in charge of me.

I quickly checked inside my right front pocket to feel my last bit of ammunition. I counted the three berries and brought my hand out into the open. The last three chinaberries were captured in the palm of my hand. I hurriedly sorted through the three. One was slightly yellow but firm. I dropped the other two back into my pocket. The one I had chosen, I sat carefully in the end of the barrel and with the popper pushed it halfway down the barrel of the gun. It fit snugly, which meant lower risk of a bad shot.

As Effie rounded the corner of the kitchen, I was hidden behind the chinaberry tree. The tree that had given me my berry for the last shot of the season was providing me with my coverage. I stood still, waiting for what seemed to be an eternity for Effie to walk out into the open, but as usual, Effie was in no hurry.

I slowly circled the tree to match her walk, staying fully protected and hidden. She passed by, looking for me in front of her, never thinking I was lurking behind. As she moved, stepping and dragging, I moved from behind the tree. My target was close at hand and clear. I brought the gun to my chest, held it firmly in my left hand, and with my right hand open, thrust the palm of my hand against the popper. The last berry of the season shot forth and straight as Mama's clothesline, flew through the late-summer air, and struck Effie in the center of her back.

Effie turned quick as a cat, saw me standing with my gun raised, and without a word picked up her pace, walked quickly around the corner, up the front steps, and disappeared into her room behind a closed door that closed her in and me out.

I stood covered in my shame. My gun was in hand, and two softening, yellowing chinaberries sat snugly in my right front pocket. I would have my gun for another season—I knew that—but what about my friend? I wasn't sure. I turned and walked the short distance to my house, carrying my initialed gun, two leftover chinaberries, and lots of shame.

Watch Out for Rattlesnakes

Fear

In the presence of darkness, one tends to create what is not. In the presence of light, one tends to see what is.

The LORD is my light and my salvation—whom shall I fear? The LORD is the stronghold of my life—of whom shall I be afraid? (Psalm 27:1)

There is no fear in love. But perfect love drives out fear. (1 John 4:18a)

My mama lived with a high level of fear. Perfect love might cast out fear for God, but for my mama, perfect love held on to fear. Nine children to protect and keep safe are reason enough to fear: driving trucks and tractors; racing homemade stock cars down steep, wooded hills; swimming and diving off of bridges into the dark waters of Peterman Creek; boating and fishing in Daddy's six-acre pond; sibling fights that often escalated into serious war; and poisonous snakes that crawled under plum trees and slept under peanut vines. They were real. We seldom left Mama's presence that she did not remind us to watch out for something or to be very careful. It became so common that we missed her words and forgot her advice. One of her favorite reminders was "An ounce of prevention is worth a pound of cure."

My older brothers drove trucks and plowed with tractors, causing her to fear accidents for them. For me, the one who kept the farm workers supplied with fresh spring water, her fear was rattlesnakes. My dad, who feared nothing, reminded me that snakes are afraid of people and when they hear you coming, they run away. Ease told me the same thing but was quick to say that if you stepped on a sleeping snake, the snake would bite. Rattlesnakes run, but they bite, and when they bite, they intend to kill. Their two fangs make holes that let the poisonous venom in and kill their prey. Since I walked in one of their favorite places to hide and to sleep, underneath peanut vines, Mama warned me hard and often. Fear would last for a short time and then disappear. Barefoot in the sand felt good to a boy's small feet but made Mama's fear even greater.

Killed rattlesnakes made you famous in Henry County. The *Abbeville Herald* had a summer spot on one of its inside pages for pictures of those who killed rattlesnakes. The bigger and longer the snake and the greater the number of rattlers, the more publicity went to the person or persons in the picture. It was almost like an ongoing contest. The only prize was the picture in the weekly paper. The pictures in the paper, the circulating stories about who had gotten bitten, and Mama's fear made me careful but not safe.

Mama's fear was grounded in reality. Sport, my oldest brother, was bitten by a rattler and had to be rushed to the Shell Medical Clinic for shots of the snake's venom that was collected and used to counter the poison in the bite. My brother was left with a badly infected wound. With time he healed and survived. So did Mama's fear—but at a higher level.

Effie and Panella did not worry about rattlesnakes. Panella's dark cloud kept her out of the fields and at home, and so did Effie's fits and crippled foot. Occasionally, she and I would see a green snake or a rat snake under the plum bushes or crawling around under the barn, but we did not fear rattlesnakes. I only feared them in the peanut field. My mama made sure of that! My dad would occasionally feed my mama's fear. He would reach into the back of his truck and lift up a six-foot rattler that he had shot with the rifle he kept in his truck. He would count the number of rattlers, holding them with his fingers, shaking them to remind us of his kill and what a live rattler sounded like when it was crowded or approached. One time my dad got his picture in the *Abbeville Herald*. In the picture my dad and the snake are the same height.

Merkate was Effie's second-oldest sister. While Queen was one who cleaned and cooked, Merkate worked in the fields. She was large-boned and strong; Queen was thin and petite. One time when I rode on the back of my brother's bike, I forgot and stuck my heel in the spokes. Merkate rushed to the accident, picked me up, and carried me in her arms up the hill to my house. While Queen was golden brown, Merkate was dark black.

In late spring my brothers would till the soil and, at the right time, plant the peanuts. When the peanuts sprouted and cuddled in the rows like little baby chicks huddled in the morning sun, my brothers would plow the peanuts, driving carefully so the plows would uproot the weeds growing near the peanuts, leaving the peanuts to grow without having to share the nutrients in the soil with the weeds. The weeds and grass that grew near or in the peanuts that could not be reached by the plows had to be hoed out by the farmhands. Merkate and Ease hoed from sunup to sundown.

Later, when the peanut vines began to run and cover the spaces between the rows, Merkate and Ease would pull the weeds that had escaped the plows and hoes. The weeds stood taller than the peanuts, making the weeds easy to spot and to be pulled. When it was weed-pulling time, the peanut field changed from a field of green runners separated by gray, sandy soil to a field covered with a solid green carpet. It was the green carpet that made for the feared rattlers a safe place for crawling and a cool shade for sleeping.

Merkate and Ease had gotten up before sunrise, eaten some of Queen's homemade biscuits with fried fatback, packed some of the biscuits with homemade jelly, filled a gallon jug with fresh water from the well, and arrived at the peanut field in front of Aunt Sally's as the sun peeped over the distant hill. It was a weed-pulling day, and since weeds could be easily spotted and pulled, they were the only farmhands needed for the last task before the peanuts were left undisturbed to grow till harvest.

Merkate and Ease moved at the same speed as Effie, slow and slower. The walk from their house to the peanut field was a mile and a half. Ease preferred to walk in his shoes, but Merkate liked to feel the cool sand, cooled by the night air. She wore old shoes that were worn and enlarged so she could easily step into and out of them. When they walked over the red clay, she wore shoes; but when the clay gave way to the soft, sandy soil, she would step out of her shoes, carrying her shoes in one hand and her lunch in the other. When she and Ease reached the shallow flowing branch that ran across the road, she would step out of her shoes and pause for several minutes in the cool, flowing waters while Ease stepped across the stream and moved on down the road. After enjoying her pause, Merkate would hasten her pace, quickly catching up with her pa. Walking in a hushed silence, moving toward a task that would pay wages to purchase food and maybe a new pair of shoes, Merkate prized her one-on-one time with her pa.

When they arrived at the field, Merkate picked out a clean spot on one of the terraces, stepped out of her shoes, and placed them side by side so that when the sand got too hot or when the day's work was finished, she could walk directly to them and use them to protect her feet or retrieve them for her walk home.

Pulling weeds is unlike hoeing weeds. Hoeing requires one to follow the row from beginning to end and then follow the next row back, moving across the field till each row is hoed. Weeding requires one to cover an area back and forth across the field until all the tall weeds are pulled. There's not much danger for rattlesnakes when hoeing, but the risks increase significantly for weed-pulling. Ease, like my dad, was not prone to fear, so he and Effie never talked about rattlesnakes.

It was a hot, late-summer day. Ease and Merkate had pulled the weeds from most of the peanut field that lay directly in front of Aunt Sally's house. Aunt Sally was my daddy's sister and one of my favorite aunts. In the early part of summer, when the peanuts were sprouting and the field hands were hoeing, I climbed the short, wire fence, walked across the road through her front yard, and used the faucet on the back of her house to fill my two water jugs. When she was not napping or busy with housework, Aunt Sally would open the screen door on the back of her porch and give me a handful of cookies or one of her famous fried peach pies. I learned to time my water visits far enough from lunch time or prior to her early afternoon siesta to increase my chances of receiving one of her gourmet prizes. Uncle Bill, her husband, was my bus driver.

The peanut vines had covered the spaces that separated the rows so that Ease and Merkate were walking on soil they could not see. Occasionally, a rabbit or a field mouse would dart from under their feet. Ease would let out his famous growl, "god-durn-it," and would use his hat to frighten them away. Merkate would let out a shrill scream when she was frightened by a field mouse. She was less scared of rabbits.

It was mid-afternoon when Ease noticed an area of the peanut field that was covered with beggar lice, a tall weed that spread its seeds by sticking to our clothing. Oftentimes when we would get home, Mama would help us pick off the sticky seeds one at the time until our pants were free from beggar lice. Ease was pulling other weeds as he made his way to the beggar lice. As he walked over the peanut vines, he suddenly heard a sound that signaled danger. The rattlers were loud and clear, indicating that he was too near the rattlesnake. Instead of escaping, the snake felt attacked. As Ease looked down, the rattlesnake had bowed its back, lifted its head, and quickly buried its fangs in the calf muscle of Ease's left leg. Sharp, excruciating pain swept through Ease's body.

After using his hoe to kill the snake, and not prone to either fear or anxiety, Ease took the red bandanna that he wore around his neck to catch sweat and that he used occasionally to wipe the sweat from his face and tied it around his leg above the two holes left by the penetrating fangs. He pulled it tightly to cut off as much of the circulation as he could to slow down the blood mixed with venom going to his heart. Reaching into his pocket, Ease took out his sharp pocket knife and cut an X in the middle of each hole. He brought his leg up to his mouth and sucked the poisonous venom from the calf of his leg. He calmly told Merkate to fetch her shoes, waited for her to return, explained to her what had happened, and the two of them walked the mile and a half home. As they neared the house, Ease told Merkate to run up to my house and see if Blackie could take him to the hospital in Fort Gaines, Georgia, six miles away.

When Blackie heard Merkate say that her pa had been bitten by a rattler, he jumped into Dad's empty-bodied truck and sped down the hill and found Ease waiting, sitting on the front porch steps. Blackie threw open the passenger door of the truck and demandingly urged Ease to pick up his pace and get in the truck. Fast but not reckless, Blackie drove up the hill, sped past our house, and reached the river road that ran beside the store. Increasing the speed, he drove on. Ease said to Blackie, "God-durnit, son, you are driving too fast. You gonna kill both of us before the snake kills me."

In record-breaking time, freed from the speed limit by a life-saving emergency, Blackie reached the hospital, pulled up near the emergency room, rushed in, and exclaimed and explained that he had brought a man who had been bitten by a rattlesnake to the hospital. Ease slowly walked into the hospital, climbed on a gurney, and the nurse wheeled him off to get shots of the venom to save his life. Blackie sat in the waiting room anxiously. He did not know if Ease would live or die. Soon, Dr. Quattlebaum walked into the waiting room. He told Blackie that Ease had saved his own life by sucking the venom from his leg and by staying calm. The doctor said he would keep Ease for several days because the poisonous venom would make an ugly sore. It would need to be medicated and watched to keep down the infection. Blackie left Ease lying in his bed on the colored wing of the hospital with nothing on but a hospital gown. He was smiling and enjoying the attention. Blackie looked back over his shoulder as he left the room and lifted a hand to say goodbye. Ease waved back, and Blackie walked to the truck, parked under a sycamore tree, and drove to Ease's house to tell Panella and the girls that Ease was going to be fine but would be in the hospital several days for his leg to heal. The following morning, Blackie drove Queen and Merkate to the hospital and sat in the truck while they visited with their pa and were reassured that he was going to survive and fully heal.

Having heard Blackie's detailed report to my dad about what had happened to Ease, I walked down the hill to check on Effie, knowing I would get a different report from her. Effie was sitting on the floor of her room playing with Dolly. She didn't look anxious or worried like I would have if my pa had been bitten by a rattler. I asked her if she wanted to dig for some doodlebugs. She sat still in her silence. After some time she put Dolly to bed, used the cane-bottom chair to pull up, and walked toward the door and out on the porch without saying a word. Then I knew Effie was bothered. She was not ready to talk. Soon she would be.

We walked down the front steps, looked and found sharp-pointed sticks for digging, and crawled under the porch to dig doodlebugs. Still silent, just sitting in a different place, she began to dig and to sing, "Doodlebug, doodlebug, your house is on fire. Doodlebug, doodlebug, your house is on fire." Bending over the doodlebug house, Effie reached down and plucked the doodlebug from its house and placed it in the palm of her hand. Holding it seemed to give her comfort. She reached out to me, I opened my hand, and she gently laid the doodlebug in my hand for observation and safe-keeping.

As we sat under the raised portion of her porch in silence, digging for more doodlebugs, I knew Effie wanted to talk. Like my dad's well pump that needed to be primed for the water to flow, Effie needed to be primed. I needed to ask one of my questions. "How is Ease?" I asked. My question primed the pump, and Effie told me the whole story and ended by saying that her pa was going to be fine.

I had more questions. "Effie, why did God make rattlesnakes?" I asked.

"To eat up all the rats," she answered.

"But why do they kill when they bite?"

"If they are hungry for something bigger and better than rats, their poison kills the rabbit. Then they can take their time swallowing the rabbit whole! The snake's mouth is wider than its throat, so it has to work hard to push the rabbit down to the stomach. Once it reaches the stomach, the snake can sleep and rest while it digests its dinner."

"Why did the snake bite Ease?" I asked.

"He got too close. Just like God gave dogs teeth to bite for their protection, God gave rattlesnakes fangs and poison for their protection and survival. If you get too close or make them scared, they bite."

Effie's pump was running, her water was flowing, and we were talking about things other than Ease and rattlesnakes. "Doodlebug, doodlebug, your house is on fire," Effie sang as we dug for more doodlebugs. Several days later, Ease came home, and things at Effie's house and mine were back to normal—including Mama's fear of rattlesnakes.

If It's Big Enough to Bite, It's Big Enough to Keep

Learning

To use what one knows to help another is a gift. To teach another what one knows is a gift forever.

Early in the morning, Jesus stood on the shore, but the disciples did not realize that it was Jesus. He called out to them, "Friends, haven't you any fish?"

"No," they answered.

He said, "Throw your net on the right side of the boat and you will find some." When they did, they were unable to haul the net in because of the large number of fish. (John 21:4–6)

When the hour came, Jesus and his apostles reclined at the table. After taking the cup, he gave thanks and said, "Take this and divide it among you." He took the bread, gave thanks and broke it, and gave it to them, saying, "This is my body given for you; do this in remembrance of me." (Luke 22:14, 17, 19)

Mary Kate, or Merkate as we called her, was the boy Ease never had. She was with Ease when he was bitten by the rattlesnake. She used his ax to cut down trees. She was her dad's saw partner when they used a crosscut saw to cut thick, long trunks of trees into smaller pieces that were split for firewood to be used in the kitchen stove or in one of the several fireplaces in the house. When the two of them sawed, it was like watching two persons in a tug-of-war. She would pull, and he would follow. He would pull, and she would follow. Beads of sweat would form on her forehead, puddle and run down her nose, and fall off to the ground, much like a dripping faucet. It was usually Ease who would say, "Let's take a rest."

Merkate dressed like Ease. She wore overalls and denim work shirts most of the time. Occasionally she wore a dress, usually for church on Sunday. Ease wore his Sunday clothes better than Merkate. Merkate looked like a pulpwooder in a dress. The dress had a hard time settlin' anywhere! Her shoulders were so broad that the dress fit like one of Mama's rubber gloves. Her stomach always looked pregnant. In order to cover her stomach, her dress had to hang shorter in front and longer in back. This caused her white slip to show and always made me think of what my daddy said to Mama when her slip was showing: "Sal, it's snowing!"

Merkate never acted like she thought she was pretty, even when she was dressed in her Sunday best. The frown she carried was a sign of her discomfort and clearly indicated her preference for overalls and denim shirts. The best part of Sunday for her was getting home and changing clothes. Merkate did not fit Sundays, but she did Saturdays. That was especially true in fall, when all the crops were in and Saturdays were more like a holiday.

There were the chores that never took a break, like bringing in stove wood, feeding Molly the mule, milking the cow, washing the clothes. The seasonal work was over, and the time no longer used for working made room for play. Fishing was Merkate's favorite play. It was serious play when she was hungry for fried fish and cornbread. When she took Effie and me fishing, it was just play. Only occasionally would she take us with her. We wanted to go more often than she asked.

When she took Effie and me fishing, it was always in the creek that ran quietly at the foot of the open meadow that sat directly in front of our house. Sometimes the fishing trips were planned, but there were other times when they were spontaneous. When she was hungry, she fished alone. When she wanted to show off her fishing skills or when she wanted company, she invited us. The creek ran shallow in most places, and you could stand on the bank and see the fish dart back and forth as if they were playing tag. Where the beavers made their dams or where trash collected in the stream, deeper wells of water were made, and that was the home of the fish Merkate wanted to catch, especially the bigger ones! Merkate knew where all the best fishing holes were located in the creek, and she would waste no time getting to her favorite one—the one where she had the most luck!

This particular fishing trip was planned. Merkate needed a new fishing pole, and she thought it was time for Effie and me to have ours. She used the promise of fishing as a way to get us to go to the cane grove to choose a new pole. She had used some of her cotton-pickin' money to buy the fishing line, lead weights, cork stoppers, and hooks. The same cane grove that furnished poles for the barrels of our pop guns grew tall, straight, flexible fishing poles.

Effie and I had not talked about our pop guns since my last shot. The coolness and distance that had lingered for a while slowly slipped away and dissolved. Merkate was taking us to the same grove Queen had taken us to. The cane grove at first made me feel my shame all over again. I checked with Effie out of the corner of my eye, and she seemed fine. I had learned that when bad is done to a friend, the doer suffers more than the receiver. There are some good remedies for shame—like time—but the best remedy is fishing!

On this trip to the cane grove, it seemed that I needed to have a pole bigger and longer than Effie. Maybe it was the boy thing, or maybe I was beginning to be more competitive. Merkate saved me from my lack of wisdom by not letting me make an unwise choice. Fishing in a creek that flowed beneath an arc of hardwood trees would require a short pole, not a long one. The creek was thin in most places, and the sandbars that formed where the creek bent either to the left or the right made a short pole more accessible and more appropriate.

Effie seemed to know all of that and quickly chose a short pole while I was still checking out the grove. I kept looking and looking.

Merkate finally had to tell me to pick a short pole. Her help made me feel younger and inexperienced. She did it confidently, out of her knowledge and experience; and quietly, not wanting to make me feel little. She did not rush us, knowing how important it was for Effie and me to choose our own poles. It was hard for us to stand in the midst of so many and choose just one. Finally, we did!

Merkate, like Queen, cleared away the underbrush with her ax, making way for a full, clean swing. Each of our canes fell quickly and softly. We dragged them out into the open space, and Merkate trimmed away the smaller branches. We carried them up to Effie's house to be fully dressed for fishing. Since I had chosen a shorter pole, I laid it across my shoulders and held it tightly behind my neck with both hands. It was strange how quickly a cane pole changed from one of many to a prized possession when chosen and made your own. As it sat on my shoulders and we climbed the hill to Effie's house, I imagined that the cane pole and I had grown up knowing that one day we would be partners in fishing.

Merkate was careful not to trim the very top of our cane poles. The top was so thin that I could hardly see the very end. Merkate told us to keep the top because it would make fishing more fun. I didn't understand at the time, but I would soon enough. She carefully trimmed each branch off the pole, leaving scars up and down the poles. There were thin rings that faded into the poles about every foot or so. Merkate told us that each ring was for a year of growth. I counted the rings on my pole, and it was the same age as I was. That made my pole and me even closer!

Merkate took a small brown paper bag from her overall pocket. She poured out the contents on the clean, gray dirt underneath the chinaberry tree. She picked up the clear fishing line wound tightly around a piece of thick, brown cardboard. She unwound the fishing line, measuring it against the length of each of our poles, reached into her pocket for her knife, and cut two pieces of line to match the length of each of our poles. Effie's pole was bigger and longer than my pole. She tied the line to the end of Effie's pole, using a double knot. She pulled the knot tight, cutting off the two short ends of the line. She held the pole in one hand and the line in the other to check out its feel and laid both down, obviously satisfied.

Reaching into her small paper sack, Merkate carefully took out a small hook that was about a half-inch long. She held the end of the line between her thumb and forefinger and the hook between the fingers on her left hand. Holding the line and the hook up to the light, like Aunt Vera threading her needle when she was ready to sew, Merkate stuck the line through the eye of the gray hook, pulling it until several inches of line fed through the small eye of the hook. She tightened the line, twisting it between her fingers. She pulled the end of the line through the opening at the neck of the twisted line, tied it in a double knot, and pulled on the hook to make sure the line was secure.

Effie's fishing pole was almost ready. It had a line and hook but no stopper. Store-bought fishing poles came already made, and they had a bright red stopper that floated on top of the water, directly above the weighted hook. The stopper could be adjusted by pulling it up or down the line, depending on the depth of the fishing hole. When the stopper began moving in the water, going under, disappearing out of sight, it was time to jerk the pole, causing the hook to catch in the lip of the fish and then landing it on the bank for keeps.

Merkate had no store-bought stopper. She reached into her wide pocket at the top of her overalls, pulling out several pieces of dry cane that she had picked up unnoticed when we were choosing our poles. She reached and got a stiff piece of wire and pushed the soft fiber out of the cane pieces. Forgetting that she had tied the hook to the line before threading the line through the cane stopper, Merkate quickly cut the hook off the line. She fed the line through the cane stopper and retied the hook to the line, again pulling the knot secure. She pulled the stopper down the line about two feet. Reaching into her overall pocket again, she retrieved several matches, broke them in half, and stuck a piece of the match into the hole in the cane stopper, creating enough tension so that the stopper would remain in place and not slip up or down on the line without help. She picked up Effie's pole, held the line taut, and moved the cane stopper up and down on the line until she was satisfied. She left the stopper about two feet above the hook, knowing that two feet was the right depth for the best fishing hole in the creek.

After dressing all three of our poles with line, lead weight, hook, and stopper, Merkate was eager to teach her two novice students the art of fishing. She picked up her pole, held it in her right hand, grasped the hook with her left hand, and with a gentle jerk on the pole sent the hook flying out as far as it could go. She practiced a few times as a way to teach her students that practice might not make perfect, but it would make better. She wound the line around her pole, stuck her hook in the open end of the cane pole, and gently leaned it against the side of the smokehouse. Since each pole was of a different length, she practiced on each to give us confidence that our poles were of equal quality and efficiency. Effie and I practiced our jerks until we were better with distance and aim. Soon, three poles leaned against the smokehouse, one long, one medium, and the other short. The poles, just like our guns, needed ammunition!

Merkate got up from her chair and walked toward the smokehouse. She unlatched the heavy wooden door to the small house that Ease used in late fall to smoke his country hams after hog-killing time. He built a fire that smoked more than it blazed in the dirt floor. When the house was not smoking, you could open the door and fetch the garden tool needed for different tasks. Merkate reached in and got the hoe that she used to hoe peanuts. The door hung on two rusty hinges and grunted when it was opened. With hoe in hand, Merkate led, and Effie and I followed.

Walking near but behind, we followed Merkate silently. On the farm when important tasks are being done, talking is a distraction, unless it is telling someone how to do something new or better. She led us out to the burned-off place where trash was buried or burned. She dug around in the charred remains until she found two large tin cans. The labels had been burned off, leaving us to guess what was once inside. She handed a can to Effie and then one to me.

We followed Merkate to the side of the barn to a low area that stayed wet most of the time. Coffee grounds were mixed with the wet soil to create a breeding ground for wigglers, the favorite food for the fish that swam in the creek. Merkate kept wide planks over the low area to keep the soil wet and to protect the wigglers from the hens and rooster.

As we waited for her to dig the worms, the smelly odor made us want to leave. The worms needed for fishing kept us waiting. Merkate laid down her hoe, moved the heavy planks over to the side, retrieved her hoe, and approached the wet dirt that had been dug in before. Effie and I stood close by but out of the reach of Merkate's hoe, clasping our empty cans.

I guessed that my can had housed tomatoes and her can pork-and-beans. She forced the hoe into the soft dirt and lifted a clump and laid it near Effie. "Put that in your can for the worms," she firmly said. She did the same for me. Both of our cans were now ready for the fill. Merkate wanted us to keep the worms alive and wiggling.

After pulling away the loose dirt with her hoe, Merkate raised the hoe high above her head and brought it down, cutting as deeply as she could into the undug dirt. Pulling the wet clumps up and breaking them apart with her hoe, wiggling worms would fall out of the dirt or hurry up to hide the exposed part of their body back in the dirt. At first she reached down and picked up the worms or broke apart the dirt to find the hidden ones. After placing several worms in our cans, she dug up the worms and let us shake them out of the loose soil. The first one Effie picked up wiggled, and Effie jumped back in fear. In order to advertise my manliness, I covered my fear and picked up the first one Merkate laid at my feet.

After multiple digs our cans were full of worms. Enough for three fishermen! Merkate laid down her hoe, placed the wide planks over the wet, loose dirt, returned the hoe to the smokehouse, and told us to wait under the chinaberry tree. The ground under the tree was firm and clean. More comfortable with the wiggle worms, we both dumped our cans and one by one caught the worms, counting to see how many worms were in our can. One, four, seven, fifteen, thirty was my count. The count for Effie was twenty-three, thirty, thirty-three. She had three more than I, but I knew that if I ran out of worms, Effie would share her worms with me.

Merkate had fished in the creek most of her life, so she knew exactly where to go. The open hole in the bend of the creek south of the farm road that ran through the creek had a yellow sandbar and more clear space. The trees hung back, leaving some open space in the canopy created by the branches for some blue sky and less hazard for hooks flung by novice students of the sport. Merkate left her dressed pole lying on the bank of the creek. She delayed her love of fishing so she could help Effie and me undress our poles, bait our hooks, and get ready for our first catch. Small minnows, no bigger than our worms, swam near the shore, darting back and forth as if to tease us into games that would keep us from catching brothers and sisters bigger and older than they. On other occasions we had come to the creek to play their game of "catch me if you can," but that was not our intent for the day. The game today was more serious. We had been promised fried fish, hot skillet cornbread, and new homemade cane syrup. If the bigger fish would eat our worms, we would eat them!

Effie got her hook baited first. Merkate showed her how to hook the wiggling worm several times so that the worm would be a greater challenge to the fish to eat without getting hooked. Merkate helped Effie swing the line across the creek, landing the wiggler near the deep, dark water where the larger fish hung out. As soon as it hit, the floating reed disappeared. Effie snatched her line quick and hard. Flying upward toward the branches in the overhanging trees, her hook got caught on one of the branches dressed in dark green leaves. Merkate pulled gently on the line, bending the tender branch her way until she caught it in her hand and easily loosened the hook. She baited the hook again, and Effie returned to fishing.

No more quick bites gave Merkate time to bait my hook, getting me ready to fish. Wisely, she walked me down the creek away from Effie. She knew two fishermen learning how to fish needed space. She let me hold the pole but stood behind me, helping me guide my line away from the tree branches and toward the darker water across the creek. As soon as my bait hit the water, the reed float moved through the water and disappeared. Afraid to do what Effie had done, I let it go too long, and the float reappeared and sat still in the water. As if she knew without having to see, she told me to lift the pole, raising the line higher. The hook was clean and empty. The fish had won, and I had lost. Merkate was quick to encourage, telling me that fishing is like baseball: if you catch one out of three, that is a good average.

Merkate reached into my tomato can, dug into the wet dirt, and got a new worm. She baited my hook, and I flung the line out into the creek, landing it near enough to the deep water that she left me and walked back to where Effie was fishing. Teaching us to be patient, Merkate said, "Creek fish are smart. Once you miss one, you have to wait a while before they come back to bite. They can't stay away too long. Those wiggly worms look too good hanging there in the dark, brown water."

Sure enough, Merkate was right. After a short wait Effie's float bobbed up and down, slowly picking up speed as it moved through the water and disappeared. This time, Effie's jerk was half what it was the first time.

Her jerk caught the hook in the upper lip of the fish, and she watched as her pole bowed humbly down. Merkate talked Effie into her first catch, and Effie pulled the small brim out of the water and landed it on the grassy bank. Effie's brim was flipping and flapping, trying to get the hook out of its mouth and get back into the water. Merkate left it alone for a time and then reached down with her fingers, catching the fish underneath its two gills, careful not to get finned.

The fish was a lot smaller than its pull. It was about the size of my two fingers squeezed close together. I had watched my brothers as they fished in our pond, and they only kept the bigger fish. "Too little to eat," I thought to myself.

"Is it too little to keep?" Effie asked.

Merkate quickly and firmly answered, "If it's big enough to bite, it's big enough to keep."

"What do we do now?" I asked myself, not wanting to challenge Merkate's "keeping fish" policy. The small fish had given up its last kick and lay there in the grass, seemingly resigned to the trouble it had gotten into by opening its mouth. A little fish in the creek is different from one caught and lying on the bank. I felt sorry for the little fellow and wanted to ease it back into the creek with my foot. The growing compassion I felt was overruled by Merkate's plan to keep everything that we caught. "How do we keep him from drying out?" I thought. We didn't have any salt to salt it down like those fish that come in five-gallon cans at the store. Dad called them salty fish. We had our two small cans, but they were full of worms. In our cans fish could eat but not swim!

Lying there on the bank, too tired to flip and flap, having eaten one worm, it didn't want another. Merkate walked off from the bank of the creek, broke off a thin, long branch of a sweetgum tree, and was stripping off the leaves as she walked back toward us. The little fish, thirsty for a drink, lay as still as death on the grassy bank. She reached down, picked it up, and held it tightly by the head. She opened its small mouth on its big head, stuck the thin, clean branch through its gill out through its mouth, gently pulling the stick through until the little fish rested against the Y that had been made on the branch by leaving the smaller branch attached to the bottom of the limb.

Now the little fellow was not only thirsty, but it had a sweetgum branch coming out the side of its head. Merkate stepped down from the bank onto the smooth yellow sandbar and stuck the long end of the stick into the side of the creek bank just above the water, carefully letting the fish submerge into the creek water. That was better than lying on the bank. The little fish could swim again even though it could not go anywhere. It must have felt like I did when Mama would say, "You can go outside, but you can't leave the yard." I was free, but I wasn't!

I had to get over my fish compassion and get back to fishing. A good fisherman does not get too close to his fish. If my compassion surfaced so strongly when I caught them, how could I clean and then eat them? The ones packed in salt at my daddy's store did not bother me when Daddy caught them, bagged them, and weighed them so that Willie Gene could take them home and fry them for supper. I think the difference in my compassion was that the salty ones were dead and the little creek fish was alive.

Effie caught the next two, each one bigger than the last. She had caught three and I none. Boys are supposed to be better fishermen than girls. The pressure began to build. Merkate was more interested in catching more fish to clean and to eat. Yet she knew I needed to catch one, so she moved over my way. "Let's try over here," she said. My line was sitting too close to us. She knew creek fish were too smart to be seen. Reaching over, she took my cane pole in hand and softly lifted my line with float, lead, and bait and landed it close to the other bank in deeper, darker water.

The cane float sat still for a second. Quickly, the float moved through the water and disappeared. I jerked and knew I had hooked a big one. I kept the line tight and the end of my cane pole bent toward the water. The tip of the pole, like my float, was under the water. I felt the tremor of the pull and watched as my line zigged back and forth, cutting the dark creek water like a streak of lightning cuts through the sky. Suddenly, the line quit moving. The pole stopped shaking, and my pulls caused the line to get tight.

"Wait," cried Merkate in a much stronger voice. "It's gotten tangled around one of the roots of a water oak that grew near the bank of the creek, hanging its arms across it and its feet in it. Give it some slack!"

I stepped toward the creek, loosening the line, giving whatever I had hooked some slack. My cane float reappeared. Then it was gone again, heading downstream. I raised my pole, tightening the line, gaining control of my catch. Merkate backed off and left me to do battle on my own. It was time for me to be a real fisherman. I pulled him nearer the bank and stepped back to give myself leverage to lift my catch out of the water and land it on the bank. It was the biggest one yet, a fish about the size of my hand. It was dark on top and golden yellow underneath. "A shell cracker," yelled Merkate.

Catching the big one made my excitement so high I lost my compassion. The fish lying on the bank looked so caught and so helpless. It was the helplessness that retrieved my compassion. Merkate handled that with one quick stroke. She picked up my fish by the head, fetched the long sweetgum branch, and threaded it through its open gill and large mouth. Back in the creek, out of sight and out of mind, I baited my empty hook and returned to fishing. The long sweetgum branch was beginning to fill. "Won't be long before we have a mess of fish," said Merkate.

Most fishermen run out of worms long before the creek runs out of fish, and that was true for us. There is always one more catch. The easiest way to stop fishing is to run out of worms. The last wiggler was on my hook. Effie had caught the most, and Merkate wanted me to catch the last. I had caught the biggest one, and I had fished enough with my brothers to know that biggest fish trumped more fish. Merkate and Effie pulled in their cane poles and waited for me to catch a last one.

I had developed my expertise in casting so that I landed my last worm in the very center of the deepest water. The worm was big and alive and the place perfect for a last catch. Soon, my cane cork bobbled, moved slowly downstream, and then quickly disappeared. I waited and then gave the pole a catching jerk. The biggest fish of the day had begun to eat its lunch. When I jerked, the lunch was gone, and the fish was missing. It was a good meal for a fish smart enough to eat without getting caught. I remarked that it had to be the biggest fish of the day, and Merkate wisely handled my need to exaggerate by quickly saying, "If you don't land them you, can't count them."

Wigglers all gone, it was time to quit. Without saying a word, Merkate showed us how to wind our lines around our poles and fasten the hook in the hollow end of our poles. First, she cleaned her hook of any remains from the worms and dipped the hook several times in the swiftly moving creek to remind us that clean hooks won't rust. Effie and I dumped the dirt from our cans and rested our poles across our shoulders and followed Merkate out of the thicket to the road. The long branch of the sweetgum tree filled with fish hung by her side.

Ease and Molly, the family name for Panella, were sitting on the front porch. When they saw us, Ease slowly got up from his cane-bottom chair and met us as we turned off the road. Molly sat still and silent. Ease quickly saw the string of fish and seemed proud of our catch. Others in the house ran out to meet us, sharing in our good luck. Underneath their celebration of our catch was something I was missing. They saw caught fish as fried fish!

After they had fingered each fish and asked, "Who caught this one?" holding up the big one, we followed Merkate around the house to the back porch. Ease had built a shelf between two of the outside posts. On one end of the shelf, there was a cut-out place for one of Molly's speckled blue pans. It was a perfect fit. Standing just beyond the shelf was a hand pump that Ease had put in for drinking, cooking, and washing water. Merkate filled the pan with a few strong pumps of water and one by one took each fish off the sweetgum branch and laid them in the freshly pumped pan of water. Most of the fish had died and were stiff. A few of the last ones caught had survived, and when she laid them in the pan, they flipped their tails, knocking water everywhere. One last swim!

Since the live ones were still a job to catch, Merkate searched the water till she found a live one. "I'll show you how to do it, and then you can each clean one. If you catch them, you have to clean them!" she said, still teaching us the task of fishing. Holding the head of the fish tightly in her left hand, she reached and got one of her mama's sharp kitchen knives. My compassion returned again. I turned my head and looked away. Compassion was no problem when I was catching fish. Compassion appeared when the fish were struggling on the bank out of the water and when they were facing execution and cleaning. Merkate continued the cleaning and taught Effie and me how to clean the fish, making us complete fishermen. Soon, all the fish we had caught were cleaned and ready to fry.

I had never eaten a meal at Effie's. I had eaten a hot piece of cornbread with melted butter, a piece of sweet cake, a strip of bacon, but never a meal. My mama had never told me that I couldn't; I just knew that I shouldn't. There were certain unspoken places where our friendship stopped. The eating table was one of them. Today, however, it made no sense for me to stop! To ask for my fish and go home would have been to act like adults. I was a boy. I chose to stay.

Merkate let Effie and me pour the water into the cornmeal, taking turns stirring until the water disappeared into the meal. She dipped several tablespoons of lard from the gallon bucket into the heavy, black skillet. The heat from the wood-burning stove quickly changed the lard from a solid to a liquid. With a large spoon Effie and I took turns dipping the cornmeal out of the dish into the sizzling grease. Patting the cornmeal down to make round patties, we waited for each patty to brown on the bottom, and then we flipped each one to the other side. After browning both sides, we placed each piece of cornbread on some torn-off pieces of brown paper sack to absorb some of the grease. When all of the bread was fried and placed on one of Molly's large platters, Merkate opened the warming door on the side of the oven and placed the cornbread on one of the wire racks to keep it hot and crisp while she fried the fish.

All the grease was used for frying the cornbread, so Merkate dipped several large spoonfuls of lard out of a two-gallon bucket into the hot iron skillet. As the fish fried, each one's tail curled. Merkate used the fork to hold them down so the fish would fry flat. The dark, musty kitchen began to smell good with the savors of fried fish and cornbread. After all the fish were fried, without ringing a bell or calling for dinner, the kitchen began to fill. It was the smell, not the sound, that announced dinnertime! Merkate sat two tin platters covered with brown paper to soak up the grease and to keep the fish and bread warm in the middle of the table. Some of the family sat in cane-bottom chairs. I sat between Merkate and Effie on the long, narrow bench.

When we sat down at the table to eat, Ease and Molly were offered the platters first, and each one took a fish and a piece of cornbread. They passed the platters on to the ones beside them. Each person passed the platters on without taking fish or bread. On around they came until they got to me. What was I to do? Was this a family game? Was I to do what they had done? If so, would the platters just keep on passing? As I started to send the fish platter on, keeping the passing game going, Ease said in a soft voice, "Take one, son, and pass it on."

Standing up, Merkate pointed to the fish I had caught and said, "You caught the big one, Bobby. It's yours. Eat it."

As I ate my fish and their bread, I forgot that I was white and they were black. Ease and Molly had taken the first pieces because they were parents. I had been given the next pieces, not because I was white, but because I was their guest.

Merkate had done a good job of teaching us to fish. Occasionally, she would take us fishing. More frequently, Effie and I would head back to the creek.

"Do you think it's big enough to keep?" I would ask.

And Effie would answer with a broad grin, "If it's big enough to bite, it's big enough to keep."

Jonquils—
Impatiens—
Gardenias

Beauty

Grow a seed that you buy and you know it. Grow a seed that you find and you wonder.

Then God said, "I give you every seed-bearing plant on the face of the whole earth and every tree that has fruit with seed in it." (Genesis 1:29)

Your beauty does not come from outward adornment. Instead it should be that of your inner self, the unfading beauty of a gentle and quiet spirit. (1Peter 3:3a, 4b)

How beautiful are the feet of those who bring good news. (Romans 10:15b)

As Effie grew older, so did her wishes and wants. Flowers were one of her passions, and earning some income to help out with her needs was her duty. Miss Mary had shown some interest in Effie's flowers and had asked Effie to go with her to Fort Gaines to sell some of her plants from her flower garden. The invitation opened the door, and Effie soon found her cause: do more growing and make more money. Also, I was shooting more goals with Thomas, my school friend.

Springtime for Effie was jonquil time. Jonquils are slow and easy and seem to be in no hurry to wake up or get up—much like Effie. Once they are awake, they take their time to sit, to stand; and if winter hangs around, they often go back to bed and sleep for a time longer. Impatiens are of a different nature. They are eager to wake, to grow, to bloom, to stay awake till winter drives them inside—for Effie, that usually meant Mama's sunroom or Miss Mary's basement. Miss Mary was Effie's spring-time friend. She sold her impatiens at the plant garden in Fort Gaines. For several years Miss Mary set up her plant garden right outside the front doors of Mr. McKensie's hardware store. New customers could find them, and old customers knew where they were.

Miss Mary waited impatiently for the season to come, and Effie was in no hurry to transplant her jonquils to individual cans. Miss Mary was filling her large tomato cans with freshly dug soil from the compost pile out by the burning fire that seldom burned out. When necessary, someone would remind us of hell's burning fire that never went out.

Springtime was Effie's best time. One thing special about spring for Effie was that spring could not be coerced into coming or delayed; it came when it came. Waiting was spring's best gift. Effie liked to wait, for waiting always brought something different and better. If she waited, she seldom got less. She liked to say, "Expectation is what makes celebration."

While Effie waited for her jonquils, Miss Mary waited for her impatiens. If spring slipped in a few days early, waiting moved out, and preparation was hurried and required. Effie reasoned that if something comes that you don't wait for and you don't expect, it is like the coming of just another day; but if one waits and expects someone or something to come, it makes the day special, like Christmas or a birthday or the Fourth of July.

In winter Miss Mary and Effie got what they needed—boxes for transporting and jars for planting. In spring they got what they expected— healthy green plants that needed only time and nurture to grow into maturity. Miss Mary's and Effie's expectations were real. They wanted beautiful blooms and healthy plants. If spring stole from winter a few extra days, Effie's jonquils would yawn and stretch and lift; if winter stole them back, her jonquils turned off the alarm and slept for a few more days, losing their head start. The plants were cooperating, and the spring plant garden was ready for filling. Mr. McKensie had swept off the spot and left two bales of pine straw for Miss Mary to spread to soften the look of the plant garden.

The flowers were ready, and so were the friends. Their friendship would atrophy during late summer and long winters, but with the coming of spring came the resuscitation of their deepening friendship. Part of the quick fix of the friendship was the long hours of uninterrupted conversation during their goings and comings. Miss Mary's life was like an open book with a lost cover and many pages. Most of the pages were filled, but a few were partly filled. Sometimes new pages would need to be added for her life stories that were still going, growing, and sowing. She had plenty of stories to tell and plenty of time to tell them. Effie's stories were few, her cover was on, and her pages mostly empty. It was like a mutual admiration society. Miss Mary liked to tell, and Effie liked to listen.

The rides made them friends; the carriage gave them class! The carriage was one of a kind in its looks and functions. The two long shafts that were made to fit Pearl, Miss Mary's horse, were cut out of pine and finished with a honey pine stain that softened their appearance and made the knots look like diamonds in the wood. Pearl was a rare combination of strength and mild disposition. She and Miss Mary were partners in travel as good as Uncle Bill and Aunt Sally were partners in marriage. With the bridle Miss Mary could back Pearl into the shafts, hook them through the side pockets of her vest, and the "horse and carriage" were obviously meant for each other.

The two seats sat side by side and were handsomely covered with a dark brown leather that had softened with use. The tight, stiff leather had loosened, causing long creases to run up and down on the leather that covered the seats and backs. The seats were well-dressed but at the same time comfortable. Miss Mary had her seat, and Effie had her seat, and the two never swapped out. It was a given: Miss Mary was the driver, and Effie was a springtime companion.

The carriage had a black cloth cover that was easily portable. It was kept on most of the time, but occasionally on a summerlike spring day, Miss Mary would remove it for open-air circulation. At other times she left it off because she liked the wind blowing through her hair—east on arriving and west on leaving. Some days, showers lasted all day, and they drove with the top on. Other days, they would be caught by surprise and the showers would be on them before they could raise the top. Getting wet was the pits coming in for work, but the showers brought laughter as they drove away from town. Miss Mary stayed fixed as long as she thought some young man might be casting a longing look at the carriage as she drove Pearl through town. After crossing the narrow bridge into Alabama on her way home, fixed gave way to pleasure. To some they were the flower girls. To others they were two ladies of the court!

Effie was the young black girl with Miss Mary, and Miss Mary could stand tall and strong if someone needed protection. At times she was mother to a darker child, which friendship accepted but Southern culture strongly resisted. Miss Mary went everywhere, and Effie went nowhere. The ride over the bridge and state line expanded Effie's world a hundred times.

Miss Mary's book was without cover, and the pages were crowded with stories she told. A few pages were half-full, but most pages had writing in the margins. She had entered some new pages that could not be hooked into the metal holders. They were often casualties to the blowing winds. Her stories were written, but she knew all of them well enough to recite, not read. Most of them Effie had heard fully or partially and recognized them as she started. Whether Effie had heard it or not, if Miss Mary needed to tell her story, it had to be told. Her story today was new, and she was telling it for the first time. Effie was certain she had no former ears for this one! It was new to her, and she was eager to hear.

Usually Miss Mary delayed her storytelling until they got going and she could relax, feeling that the carriage and Pearl were in sync and she could sit and not stand, giving Pearl total control, putting the carriage on automatic pilot like they do with the big birds that fly. Effie's pa had been in the army, stationed in France, and had often talked about rides over the big water that made the Chattahoochee look like a drip from the pump when some of the water was left inside.

A story started never kept going when they moved closer to the steepest slope on highway 364. The slope was named McCrary Hill, given the name of the one who owned the acreage that included the steep hill. The hill was darkened by thick, tall, hardwood trees, casting a dark shadow over the hill, and the dense underbrush closed in the bottom so that one going by could hear but not see. Effie's pa had told the stories of overgrown bobcats and howling ghosts that lingered after death before going on to hell, they said, "'cause why would one linger if heaven were her final destination?" Lingering made sense only when there was certainty that one who lived like Mr. Pugh had no chance to gain entry above. Mr. Pugh was one of those howling ghosts 'cause he worked hard to linger as long as he could. Scaring folks was what was left, and he was quite accomplished. Pearl sensed such happenings, and Miss Mary had to be fully present when Pearl started down or up McCrary Hill.

The daily rides were refreshing and entertaining. Miss Mary's book left no stories untold. One of her stories was full of sadness, and that story was seldom told. Seated and turning to Effie, Miss Mary began, "I moved in with my sister and brother-in-law after both of my parents died. They died two months apart. I was twelve when I moved from a neighborhood to a shack of a house back deep in the woods where no one but those who live there come. In recent years Tom Wolf has moved in for short periods of time while he is marking trees for cutting. Other than church, where my sister Polly is the pianist, we don't go out much. Springtime is my time to see more, hear more, do more."

As they neared the bridge, Miss Mary closed her book and stuck it under her carriage seat, and soon they were unloading plants for the garden—jonquils with nodding heads and impatiens with curled-up lips—both plants needing the morning sun and a swig of water to lift their heads and uncurl their lips.

Miss Mary had started one of her stories that needed to be told and would be told after they crossed the river going home. The river was the stopping place for stories coming and the starting place for stories going. As soon as Pearl stepped her hoof on 'Bama soil, Miss Mary reached down and fetched her book. Before telling her story that was from her most private page, she needed reassurance that her story would be told, heard, and never retold. When she went to her private page, she always sought reassurance by extracting from Effie a promise. "Do you promise not to tell, Effie?" After stating her promise "to hear but never tell," Miss Mary would start with a verbal sprint.

"There are three men at my house: two of them live in, and the other one comes in several times each week. The two who live in are Emmett and Tom, and Willie comes to help with my flowers and to do chores on the farm with Emmett. What makes me uncomfortable is that recently Emmett looks with wistful eyes, and when I quickly turn away, he acts hurt and disappointed. He and Polly are distant in their marriage, and the marital bed is dry. Looking to someone else to find what is missing makes me cringe when the someone else is me. Then there is Tom. His wistful eyes look more often. Having stayed with us three other times, Tom has built up in his head that availability is reason enough for his wistful eyes to be met with more acceptance. What I offer back is rejection, and the anger gets more collected. Tom is a good man but not my kind of man. I'm not looking for a brother; I'm looking for a lover! Now there is Willie. I catch his wistful eye, and it doesn't ask, 'Are you only my friend?' It makes a statement: 'You are only my friend.' Three men in our house, and I have absolutely no wistful eye to offer. Emmett is jealous of Tom. Tom is angry with Emmett for what he wants. Willie is fractured and unable to keep friendships. His insecurities demand possession. Ownership! At night I push my heavy dresser against my bedroom door and sleep lightly, listening for any sounds of venture by three men I neither trust nor desire."

Miss Mary kept going with her story. She paused as they drove up McCrary Hill, and she never came back to her story. Perhaps she thought Effie's listening was saturated or her telling got too close to real. Her book closed and was stashed back under her seat. Miss Mary stood and guided Pearl to Effie's house, where Effie bid her farewell.

Miss Mary dropped Effie off late Wednesday afternoon, and Friday was to be the last day for their spring plant garden. Thursday would be sell-all day, lowering the price to almost nothing if necessary. After Thursday, Miss Mary and Effie would load up the carriage with cans full, cans empty; with blankets used to cover the plants on cool spring evenings;

with some other produce that both had brought at different times to add some change to the kitty. Effie had brought some of her dad's best peanuts, and Miss Mary had brought some of her sweet chinkapins that she had picked up under the largest chinkapin tree in the county. There was always lots to bring home, but two trips would be sufficient. As Effie walked from the road down to her house, Miss Mary and her display of angst walked with her.

The next morning was the morning before the last day of spring plant garden. Miss Mary had chosen to delay going for an hour to give her time to unload the carriage and clean it to give them a sense of party for they had good news to celebrate. Miss Mary had sold more impatiens than ever before. Effie had sold fewer jonquils but had made more money than last year. As Effie often said, "Expectations make for celebrations!"

The sun shone brightly as Effie waked to the road a little later, knowing Miss Mary would be an hour late. She had walked to the road carrying a jar of her mom's homemade fig preserves to give Miss Mary for her more-than-fair share of their business partnership that today would end their three-year anniversary. To make sure the preserves arrived safely to the road, Effie made a second trip to carry everything else she needed to take with her. Effie waited for a second hour, but Miss Mary was nowhere in sight. Effie walked down to the house to consult with Ma, and Ma called attention to Miss Mary's infrequent tardiness. However, her record was not perfect, so she told Effie to wait longer. After waiting another thirty minutes, and with no way to know why Miss Mary was late, Effie packed up her wares and turned to walk home for the fourth time.

Suddenly, Effie saw Mr. Joe's truck as it made the curve and came into full view. He drove straight to where Effie stood, giving Effie her first clue that it was about Miss Mary. If not, Mr. Joe would have turned in at his house. Rolling down his passenger-side window, Mr. Joe said words Effie could not hear. She felt pain she could not bear, yet the words would not go away. Giving her time to listen, Mr. Joe told Effie that on the way home yesterday afternoon, something had frightened Pearl, and she had broken out running. The carriage had flipped and had penned Miss Mary between the carriage and a large sweetgum tree. The force of the carriage and the stability of the tree had created a blow that Miss Mary could not take; she had been killed instantly.

Mr. Joe drove off in his truck and pulled in at his place. Effie sat down under a persimmon tree, and her mind started reeling. Miss Mary and Pearl were such a trusting team. Effie recalled the last story Miss Mary had told before she closed her book and stuck it underneath her seat: Of the three, which one?

Later that night, as Effie lay in bed, her mind continued to churn. What could have frightened Pearl into running out of control through woods that were her home? Miss Mary was too good with Pearl. If frightened, Miss Mary would have kept her on the road. Effie turned, blew out her candle, and whispered goodnight to her sister Kate.

Several days later, Mr. Joe pulled up in front of Effie's house and called Pa and Effie out to his truck. The latest news was that a pine log shaped much like a club had been found near the carriage with blood and wads of a lady's hair on it. The sheriff was called, the location was identified, and using yellow tape tied around trees, the sheriff marked a large area as off-limits. Soon, the sheriff would make a statement. Effie had made her own judgment.

Effie continued to grow her flowers and often remembered the good days across the river where flowers bloomed and she and Miss Mary were more than partners in business. They were the best of springtime friends.

One Last Gift

Memory

Memory is one of the lasting gifts of love. Memory keeps those we love within reach so that we hear their voices, see their faces, and enjoy their company. Memory keeps the creek flowing, the fish biting, the doodlebugs rising, and the lightning bugs blinking. With memory, pain is released, and joy is kept forever.

There is a time for everything, and a season for every activity under heaven: a time to be born and a time to die, a time to weep and a time to laugh, a time to mourn and a time to dance. (Ecclesiastes 3:1; 2:4)

Effie and I remained friends as long as one of us was a child. As she became more an adult and less a child, our friendship lingered, though both of us knew it was changing. Color was not the reason for the change. We had learned to live with that. I was more into sports with my brothers and my new friend Thomas. I didn't know how to keep playing with Effie. We kept going to the creek, our favorite place. We still fished, but we caught fewer darting minnows. We talked about more real things, bigger things. We dreamed less and fantasized never. We picked peas, and we dug potatoes. We gathered fewer flowers, and we waded less often in the creek. We worked more and played less. Effie didn't seem to mind. It was as if she expected it. She didn't try to hold me back or draw me closer. She, like a wise parent, let me change and grow and go and made me feel that it was right.

Something else was changing. Effie was sick more often. We didn't talk about it, but the fits happened more frequently and more harshly. She slowly gave up more and more of the outside world and joined Panella, staying inside and away. Often my invitations to go fishing or plum-picking were met with, "Come back tomorrow." I always felt that meant much later than tomorrow. It was her gentle and easy way to say No without making me feel rejected. Effie slowly withdrew from all that she had so warmly embraced and improved. She was moving in, and I was moving out, and the friendship was willing to let it happen. We had seldom been possessive, and there was no reason to be so now.

I left my small country school in Shorterville for the larger schools of Abbeville. I made the junior varsity basketball team in seventh grade. I practiced hard, for I wanted to be accepted by my new school friends, and basketball was a good way to find acceptance. In between milking and carrying in stovewood, picking the vegetables and fruits, and gathering the eggs, I shot basketball on the homemade goal Daddy and my older brothers had made for me.

The goal was made from one of the metal bands that fit snugly around a bale of cotton, and the backboard was a square cut from a piece of leftover plywood. The pole was one of Daddy's cedar trees cut from the large cedar grove down by the river. My basketball goal was not like the ones in the city, but it was a good one for the country. Thomas came over more often, and we played long and practiced hard. We got better at the game and at being best friends.

Effie got sicker. I hardly ever saw her. Even when riding by her house, going to or coming from the peanut fields, I seldom saw her outside in the yard. Occasionally, she would be sitting on one of the long benches on her front porch. Most of the time her head was bent down, and my wave drew no response. I kept up my waving and once in a while got one in return.

There was a growing silence about Effie. Somehow my parents knew, but they said nothing. I was so busy with my own life that the silence was present but seldom interpreted. When Mama finally told me that Effie had died, I took it as a fact. In the country, people and animals get sick, and they die. The country is all tied together in some ways for survival, but there is a whole lot of space. When an animal dies, it is more fact than feeling. When a white person dies, the blacks treat it as a fact. When a black person dies, it is handled as fact, and if feelings are present, they are leaked out much like the faucet hooked tightly on the side of the barn. They drip out!

It was that way for me when Mama told me Effie had died. I heard her words, picked up my basketball, and played one-on-one with myself. My feelings were buried deep, and I thought that was where they belonged.

On Saturday mornings, the farm was usually a quieter place. That particular Saturday, it was especially so. It was a hot, midsummer day. The sky was bright blue with lots of fluffy white clouds. It was a good day for dreams and fantasies, but those were left to days past. Several cars and trucks were parked at Effie's house, a rare sight. I knew what day it was. No one had said, but I had figured it out: it was Effie's funeral day. Soon, the family would get in those cars and trucks and follow the big black car that was made for the purpose of carrying bodies. It would slowly climb the hill and pass in front of our house, taking Effie for what would be her final ride.

The graveyard at St. Paul's Church was different from the ones at Pilgrim's Rest, Judson, and Old Zion. At St. Paul there were just a few white marble markers. Mostly there were wooden crosses sitting at the head of mounds of dirt that looked much like where Effie and I had helped Ease bury the cane stalks. Effie was the first in her family to die, other than little Mo. He had been buried underneath the big oak tree. She was the first one to be buried at St. Paul's.

As I had gotten older, the warm, tender feelings and memories that had been the result of our long, ongoing friendship had been firmly capped inside me and put away. They lay buried in the sandy soil of my life, much like the cane stalks buried under the mounds of soft, rich dirt down by the creek. Just as Ease had assured us that those stalks would rise again in the warm soil of summer, Effie would rise again in the sweet arms of Jesus.

On this day, Effie's last day, I sat on the porch, waiting to see Effie ride by for the last time. The big black car in which she rode topped the hill and turned onto the road that ran in front of our house. The trip to the church was about five miles. I thought, "This time Effie has a ride all the way to the church." Ease and Panella sat in the backseat of someone's car, dressed in their Sunday best. They were taking Effie as far as they could go, to St. Paul's. As the black car slowly slipped out of sight, I looked across the grassy meadow toward the creek, and good memories flashed quickly against the screen of my mind.

There were some dancing water bugs and darting minnows. Even in the bright sunlight, I saw a lightning bug flitting up then down and up again, staying safely out of reach. I heard the rollin' store that ran no more slow down and come to a stop in front of Effie's house. I saw her Christmas tree, growing tall, bumping its tall head against the bright blue sky. I heard her soft, kind voice and watched doodlebugs leave their darkness and climb upward toward the light. I could see a tear in Ease's eye and became aware of the one in my eye when it broke and slowly crawled down my cheek. As Effie rode by, so did many of the memories that had been planted deeply in the soil of our friendship, memories that would last forever.

As the last car in the slow, moving caravan moved out of sight, disappearing behind the scuppernong vines that grew beside the road, I was fast closing my book of memories when suddenly and unexpectedly a bright red cardinal flew in from the trees off to the side. It sat confidently on a branch of the mimosa tree that stood directly in front of me as I sat on the east side of the porch. He was clean and colorful, much like the one that bathed and drank from the waters of the creek. I thought Effie's thought—

brighter but not better. A warm feeling embraced me from within. "This isn't just another red bird," I concluded. "It is Effie's last gift to me."

I heard her gentle, soft, kind voice whisper, "Goodbye, Bobby. Everything's gonna be all right!" The red bird raised its wings and flew away. I picked up my basketball and dribbled toward the court while Effie moved on up the road toward St. Paul's cemetery.

"No matter what accomplishments one makes, someone helps you."
—Althea Gibson

www.ingramcontent.com/pod-product-compliance
Lightning Source LLC
Chambersburg PA
CBHW050346030726
47503CB00008B/2641